ROCKETS SLAMMED PAST

—just missing the tall, gaunt man who dodged down the stairs of the Earth Embassy. A figure loomed in a doorway and he snapped off a quick blaster shot at it—missed.

He'd killed one man, wounded others—and was carrying papers stolen from the secret Embassy files. They had to stop him—but they couldn't!

—And, worlds away, the men of Department 99 watched on their galaxy-spanning viewscreen . . . knowing they were responsible for this disaster—and powerless to do anything about it!

D-99

a science-fiction novel by

H. B. FYFE

WILDSIDE PRESS

www.wildsidepress.com

ONE

AT THE NINETY-FIFTH FLOOR, WESTERVELT LEFT the public elevator for a private automatic one which he took four floors further. When he stepped out, the dark, lean youth faced an office entrance whose double, transparent doors bore the discreet legend. "Department 99."

He crossed the hall and entered. Waving at the little blonde in the switchboard cubby to the right of the doorway, he continued a few steps into the office beyond. Two secretaries looked up from the row of desks facing him, a third place being unoccupied. Behind them, long windows filtered the late afternoon light to a mellow tint.

"Did you get it all right, Willie?" asked the dark girl to his left. "Mr. Smith wants you to take it right in. He expected you earlier."

"My flight from London was late; I did the best I could after we landed," said Westervelt. "It took me the whole day to fetch this gadget. At least let me get my coat off!"

He moved to his right, to a modest desk in an alcove formed by the end of the office and the high partition that enclosed the switchboard.

"How do you find yourself inside that?" asked the other secretary, a golden haired girl with a lazy smile. "Talk about women's clothes! The men are wearing topcoats like tents this year."

Westervelt felt himself flushing, to his disgust. He struggled out of the coat, removed an oblong package and a large envelope from inner pockets, and tossed the coat on his desk.

It had hardly settled before the door at the opposite end of the office, beyond the dark girl, was flung open. From the next room lumbered a man who looked even lankier than Westervelt because he was an inch or two over six feet tall. His broad forehead was grooved by a scowl of concentration that brought heavy eyebrows nearly together over a high-bridged nose. His chin seemed longer for his chewing nervously upon his lower lip. He was in shirtsleeves and badly needed a haircut.

"I'm going down to the com room, Miss Diorio," he told the brunette. "There's another weird report coming in!"

He vanished into the hall with a clatter.

His secretary looked at Westervelt, a smile tugging at the corners of her full lips. She threw up her hands with a little flip.

"I told you to take it right in," she reminded him.

"Aw, come on, Si! What if I'd been in the doorway when he came through?"

"What is it, anyway?" asked the other girl.

Westervelt looked around as she rose. Beryl Austin, he thought, would be a knockout if only there were less of a hint of ice about her. She was, in her high heels, only an inch shorter than he. Her face was round, but with a delicate bone structure that lent it an odd beauty. Westervelt was privately of the opinion that she spoiled the effect by wearing her hair in a style too short and too precisely arranged. *And too bleached,* he told himself.

The talk was that before coming to the Department, she had won two or three minor beauty contests. That might explain the meticulous make-up and the smart blue dress that followed the curves of her figure so flatteringly. Westervelt suspected, from hints dropped by Simonetta Diorio, that this was insufficient qualification for being a secretary, even in such a peculiar institution as Department 99. Of course, maybe Smith had ideas of making her a field agent.

He held out the package in the palm of his hand.

"They said at the London lab that it was a special flashlight that would pass for an ordinary one."

"Oh, the one for that Antares case," exclaimed Beryl. "Si was telling me how they'll send out plans of that. Did they show you how it works?"

"It gives just a dim beam until you press an extra switch," said Westervelt. "Then it puts out a series of dashes bright enough to hurt your eyes."

"What in the world do they want that for?" asked Beryl.

"What in some other world, you mean! On some of these planets, the native life is so used to a dim red sun that a flash like this on their sensitive eyes can knock them unconscious."

"This place is just full of dirty tricks like that," said the blonde. "Why can't they free these people some other way?"

Westervelt and Simonetta looked at each other. Beryl had been in the Department only a few weeks, and did not yet seem to have heard the word.

Or understood it, maybe, thought Westervelt. *She might not look half so intelligent without that nice chest expansion.*

"Some of them just get in trouble," Simonetta was saying. "The laws of alien peoples we've been meeting around the galaxy don't necessarily make sense to Terrans."

6

"But why can't they stay away from such queer places?"

"What would you do," asked Westervelt, "if you were in a spaceship that blew up near a strange planetary system, and you took an emergency rocket to land on the best looking planet, and the local bems arrested you because they have a law against anyone passing through their system without special permission?"

"But how can they make a law like that?" demanded Beryl.

"Who says they can't? They had a war with beings from the star nearest them; and wound up suspicious of every kind of spaceship. We have a case like that now."

"They've been working on it two months," Simonetta confirmed. "Those poor men were jailed over a month before anybody even heard about them."

Beryl shrugged and turned back to her desk. Westervelt watched her walk, thinking that the rear elevation was good too, until it occurred to him that Simonetta might be taking in his expression. The blonde settled herself and leaned back to stretch. He was willing to bet ten credits that she did it just to get his goat.

"Well, the work is interesting," Beryl admitted, "but I don't see why it can't be done by the Department of Interstellar Relations. The D.I.R. has trained diplomats and knows all about dealing with aliens."

"Come on, now, dear!" said Simonetta. "Where do you think your paycheck orginates? Publicly, the D.I.R. doesn't like to admit that we exist. To hide the connection, they named us after the floor we're on in this building, and hoped that nobody would notice us."

"I knew I was getting into something crooked!" exclaimed Beryl.

"It depends," said Westervelt. "Suppose some Terran spacer is slung into jail out there somewhere, for something that would never be a crime in the Solar System. The D.I.R. protests, and the bems simply deny they have him. How far can diplomacy go? We try getting him out some other way."

He held up the "flashlight."

"Now they'll stellarfax plans of this out to Antares to our field agents. After one is made and smuggled in to our case, all they have to do is run in a fast ship to pick him up when he breaks out."

"Speaking of that gadget," Simonetta suggested, "why don't you take it down to Mr. Smith? He must be waiting out the message in the com room."

Westervelt agreed. He took the package and the envelope of blueprints, and walked into the hall. He turned first to his right, along the base of the U-shaped corridor, then to

7

his left after passing the door to the fire stairs at the inner corner and the private entrance to Smith's office opposite it.

The walls were covered by a gray plastic that was softly monotonous in the light of the luminous ceiling. The floor, nearly black, was of a springy composition that deadened the sound of footfalls.

Along the wing of the "U" into which he turned, Westervelt passed doors to the department's reference library and to a conference room on his right, and portal marked "Shaft" on his left. Beyond the latter was a section of blank wall behind which, he knew, was a special shaft for the power conduits that supplied the department's own communications instruments.

The place was a self-sufficient unit, he reflected. It had its own TV equipment and a sub-space radio for reaching far-out spaceships, although most routine traffic was boosted through relay stations on the outer planets of the Solar System.

Some lines of communication with the field agents were tenuous, but messages usually got through. If the lines broke down, someone would be sent to search the confidential files for a roundabout connection.

I wonder how many of us would wind up in court if those files became public knowledge? thought Westervelt. *I'd like to see them trying to handle Smitty! Nobody here can figure him out all the time, and we're at least half as nutty as he is.*

Down beside the communications room, though normally reached by the other wing of the corridor that enclosed the core of elevators, shafts and rest rooms, the department even had a confidential laboratory. Actually, this was more in the nature of a stock room for peculiar gadgets and implements used for the fell purposes of the organization. Westervelt did not like to wander about in there, for fear of setting something off. It was more or less the domain of the one man in the department whom he knew to have been in an alien prison.

Robert Lydman was an ex-spacer who had joined the group after having been rescued from just such an incarceration as he now specialized in cracking. Westervelt had been told that the sojourn among the stars had left Lydman a trifle strange, which was probably why they no longer used him as a field agent.

He came to the blank end of the corridor, the last door on the right being that of the communications room. He opened it and stuck his head inside.

The room was dimmer than the corridor. The operators, who sometimes had to contend with much-relayed faint images on their screens, liked it that way. They kept the window filters adjusted so that it might as well be night outside. Here and there, small lights glowed at various radio receivers or tape recording instruments, and there was a pervading background rustle of static blended with quiet whistles and mutterings.

At the moment, the operator on duty was Charlie Colborn, a quiet redhead who kept a locker full of electronic gadgets for tinkering during slow periods. Smith sat near him in a straight-backed chair, watching the screen before Colborn.

A message was coming in from the Pluto relay—Westervelt recognized the distant operator who spoke briefly to Colborn before putting the message through. The next face, blurry from repeated boosting of the image, was that of a stranger.

"This is Johnson, on Trident," the man said. "Capella IV tells me they gave you the facts about Harris. That right?"

Smith hitched himself closer, so the transmitter lens could pick him up. Westervelt tip-toed inside and found himself a stool.

"We just got the outlines," Smith said. "You say this spacer is being held by the natives, and they won't let you communicate with him. Have you reported to the D.I.R.?"

The distance and the relaying caused a few seconds of lag, even with the ultra-modern subspace equipment.

"I *am* the D.I.R.," said the face on the screen, after a bitter pause. "Along with several other jobs, commercial and official. There are only a few of us Terrans at this post, you know. The natives won't even admit they have him."

"Then how can you be sure they do? And why can't you get to him somehow?"

"We know because he managed to get a message out—we think." Johnson frowned doubtfully. "That is, he did if we can believe the . . . ah . . . messenger. We made inquiries of the natives, but it is impossible to make much of an investigation because their civilization is an underwater one."

Smith noticed Westervelt.

"Willie," he whispered hastily, "get on the phone and have one of the girls stop in the library and fetch me the volume of the *Galatlas* with Trident in it."

Westervelt dropped his package on a table and punched Beryl's number on the nearest phone. Meanwhile, with its weird pauses, the interstellar talk continued.

The missing Terran, Harris by name, had insisted against all advice at the outpost on one of the watery planet's few islands, upon conducting submarine exploration in a converted space scout. Since ninety-five percent of the surface

9

of Trident was ocean, Johnson had only a vague idea of where Harris had gone. The point was that the explorer had been too long out of touch. The natives, a sea people of crustacean evolution, who were to be found over most of the ocean bottom, and who had a considerable culture with permanent cities and jet-propelled submarine vehicles, admitted to having heard of Harris but denied knowledge of his whereabouts.

"So we reported to the D.I.R. sector headquarters," Johnson concluded. "They sent an expert to coax the Tridentian officials into visiting the shallows for a conference, but nothing came of it. Then we called in one of your field agents and he referred us to you."

Beryl entered the room quietly, bearing a large book. Westervelt held out his hand for it, but she seemed not to see him until he rose to offer her the stool. When he turned his attention back to the screen, Smith was probing for information which the distant Johnson sounded reluctant to give.

"But if they deny everything, how do you know he's not dead instead of being held in one of their cities? Why do you think he's being made a sort of exhibit?"

Johnson hemmed and hawed, but finally confessed.

Besides the crustaceans, who were about man-sized and "civilized," there was another form of intelligent—or at least semi-intelligent—life on Trident. Certain large, fish-like inhabitants of the planet's seas had been contacted more than once to deliver messages to the exploring members of the outpost. This was always promptly accomplished by having one of the "fish" contact another of the same species who was in the right location.

"What did you say?" demanded Smith. "Telepathic? A telepathic fish? Oh, no! Don't ask us to—Well, what I mean is . . . well, how do you know they're reliable?"

More in the same vein followed. Westervelt stopped listening when he realized that Smith was being convinced, willing or not. Stranger things were on record in the immensity of the known galaxy, but Smith took the attitude that they were all a plot against Department 99. Westervelt pried the book from Beryl's grasp and turned over pages to the article on the planet Trident.

He skimmed the opening, which dealt with galactic coordinates and the type of star at the center of the system, and did the same with the general description of the surface and what was known of the life forms there. The history since discovery was laconically brief.

Here it is, he told himself. *A species of life resembling a Terran fish in general configuration, about twenty feet in*

10

length and suspected of having some undetermined sense whereby individuals can locate each other at great distances. Well, by the time it's in print, it's outdated.

Someone turned on a brighter light, and he realized the interstellar talk was at an end. Smith looked around. He held out his hand for the book, seeming to take for granted that someone should have found the page.

"I don't see *how* we're going to reach this one," he grunted, plopping the volume down on the table to scan the article.

Colborn snatched at a small piece of apparatus he had evidently been assembling. Only Beryl was impressed; the others knew that Smith said this of every new case.

"Tell Mr. Lydman and Mr. Parrish I want a conference," the department head requested. "We'll use the room next door."

Beryl and Westervelt left Colborn examining his gadget suspiciously and retraced their steps up the corridor. At the door to the main office, the blonde left him, presumably to go through to the corner office occupied by Parrish, whose secretary she was. Westervelt dwelt on the thought of sending her on the way with a small pat, but forced himself to continue up the other wing of the "U."

He passed two doors on his left: another conference room and a spare office used mainly for old files. Doors to his right led to washrooms. This end of the hall was not blank as on the other side; it had a door labeled "Laboratory—No Admittance." The last door to the left, corresponding to the location of the communications room, led to Lydman's office.

Westervelt knocked, waited for the sound of a voice inside, and walked in. For a moment, he saw no one, then pivoted to his right as he remembered that Lydman kept his desk on the inner wall, around the short corner behind the door. Everyone else who had a corner office sat out by the windows.

He found himself facing a heavy man whose bleached crewcut and tanned features bespoke much time spent outdoors. Very beautiful eyes of a dark gray-blue regarded him steadily until Westervelt felt a panicky urge to run.

Instead, he cleared his throat and gave Smith's message. Lydman always had the same effect upon him for the first few minutes, although he seemed to like Westervelt better than anyone else at the office, even to the point of inviting him home for weekends of swimming.

I always get the feeling that he looks right through me and back again, thought Westervelt, *but I can't see an inch into him!*

TWO

CASTOR P. SMITH SAT AT THE HEAD OF A STEEL and plastic table in the conference room, whistling thoughtfully as he waited for his assistants. Next door in the communications room, the tortured tune his lips emitted would have been treated as deliberate jamming. Simonetta Diorio entered carrying a recorder, and he roused himself for a smile of appreciation.

"You won't forget to turn it on when you start, Mr. Smith?" she pleaded.

"I'll keep my finger on the switch until then," he grinned. "Thanks, Si."

Left alone again, he told himself he would have to do something about the reputation he was acquiring—quite without foundation, he believed—for being absent minded. After all, he was hardly likely to forget to record a conference when it had been his own idea. So many ideas were tossed around on a good day that some were bound to be lost, unless they were down on tape. Even a good steno like Simonetta could not guarantee to keep up with it all when two or three got to talking at once.

Generally, he admitted to himself, he erased the tape without the necessity of filing some brilliant solution. Still, the one in a thousand that did turn up made the precaution worthwhile.

He stared morosely at the volume of the *Galatlas* he had brought from the communications room. Sometimes, in this job, he lost his sense of galactic direction. Calls were likely to come in from stars of which he had never heard.

Wish I could get a little more help from the D.I.R., he thought. *It's more than having one secretary on vacation just now; we're always short-handed. They never brought us up to strength since old Murphy blew himself up in the lab with that little redhead. Maybe Willie will grow into something. That will take years, though. We ought to have some kind of training school.*

In Smith's opinion, he should have had a larger force of full time agents in the field, but he recognized the difficulties inherent in the immensity of Terran-influenced space. Even recruiting was a hit-or-miss process. He had made various working arrangements out of chance contacts with independ-

12

ent spacers—he supposed that it was unofficially expected of him—and most had worked out well. About a dozen routine cases were currently being handled out there somewhere by a motley group of his own men and piratical temporary help. In addition, there were three hot-cases that had required supervision from headquarters.

I wonder if we should stay a little late tonight? he asked himself. *I hate to ask them again, but who knows what will break with this new skull-cracker?*

He looked up as Pete Parrish entered. His dapper assistant walked around the other end of the table and took a seat on the window side.

"I hear you have another one," he greeted Smith.

Parrish was a trim man of thirty-six or thirty-seven, just about average in height but slim enough to seem taller. Smith was aware that the other took considerable pains to maintain that slimness. By his own account, he rode well and played a fast game of squash.

The wave in his dark hair was somewhat suppressed by careful grooming. He smiled frequently, or at least made a show of gleaming teeth; but at other times his neat, regular features were disciplined into a perfect mask.

Thank God that he doesn't wear a mustache! thought Smith. *That would put him over the brink.*

He was reasonably certain that Parrish had given the idea careful calculation and stopped just short of the brink. That would be typical of the man. He had been at one time a publicist, then a salesman, on Terra and in space. Actually, he should have been a confidence man. It was not until the Department had stumbled across him that he had found opportunity to exercise his real talents. He was expert at estimating alien psychology and constructing rationalizations with which to thwart it.

Smith realized, self-consciously, that he had been staring through Parrish. He passed one hand down the back of his neck, reminding himself that he must get a haircut. He could not imagine why he kept forgetting; it occurred to him every time he faced Parrish. He decided further to wear a freshly pressed suit the next day.

Lydman padded in, glanced about the room, and sat down as near to the door as he could without leaving an obvious gap between himself and the others. He eyed Parrish briefly, and raised one hand to check the scarf at his throat. Lydman dressed unobtrusively, and probably would have preferred an old-fashioned tie to the bright neck scarves favored by current fashion.

I wonder why I get all the nuts? Smith asked himself,

13

avoiding the beautiful eyes by looking squarely between them. *Even the girls—people with romantic ideas of cloak and dagger work, or the ones that owe us favors, keep sending us peaches. Then they marry off, or go around acting so secretive that they draw attention to us.*

Sometimes, he had to admit, he would have preferred having a babe marry and leave the department. Parrish was often helpful in such situations, which was only fair since he created most of them. Twice divorced, the assistant had lost none of his interest in women. He was as clever at feminine psychology as at alien.

"Well, I suppose you've heard something of the new squawk," Smith said to break the silence. "I just don't see how we're going to reach this one. The damned fool got himself taken on an ocean bottom."

He proceeded to outline the facts so far reported. Parrish received them impassively; Lydman began to scowl. The ex-spacer developed special grudges against aliens who attempted to conceal the detention of Terrans.

"First, let's see where we are before we tackle this," suggested Smith. "I've given you enough on Harris to let it percolate through your minds while we review the other cases. It looks like something we should all be in on."

Sometimes he would put a case in the charge of one of them, but they were accustomed to exchanging information and advice.

"This business of the two spacers who were nailed for unauthorized entry in the Syssokan system seems about ripe," he reminded them. "Taranto and Meyers, you remember."

"Oh, yes," said Lydman in a withdrawn tone. "The dope."

"That's right. There was no trouble getting information about them, just in comprehending the idiot reasoning that would maintain a law that makes it a crime to crash-land on that planet. Terra, like any other stellar government, is permitted one official resident there. Fortunately, we got the D.I.R. to slip him a little memo about us before he was sent out, and this is the outcome. They may even be on the loose right now."

"Let me see," mused Parrish. "Bob gave you the formula for something that practically suspends animation, didn't he?"

"Yeah," said Lydman. "We figured on the bastards to carry the bodies out and dump them. A bunch of tramp spacers is standing by to pick them up."

"No reason why it shouldn't work," said Smith. "Variations of it have been keeping us in business. Some day we'll slip up just by relying on it too much, but this looks okay. How is your Greenhaven case coming, Pete?"

14

Parrish hesitated before answering. He stroked the edge of the table with well manicured fingertips as he considered.

"Maria Ringstad," he said thoughtfully. "These reporters should be more careful, should have some knowledge of the cultures they poke into. Greenhaven is hardly a colony to swash a buckle through. I suppose she never thought they would bother a newswoman."

"Did you ever get the answer to what she was after on Greenhaven?"

"Nothing, just passing through!" Parrish snapped his fingers in contempt. "She was on a space liner enroute to Altair VII to gather material for a book. It stopped on Greenhaven to deliver a consignment of laboratory instruments."

"Those Greenies," Lydman put in, "are as crazy as bems. What a way to live!"

"They *have* been described as the bluest colony ever derived from Terra," agreed Smith. "I shudder to think of the life Pete would lead there."

Parrish smiled, but not very deeply.

"Miss Ringstad's mistake was fairly simple-minded," he said. "They had official prices posted in that shop she visited for souvenirs. When they claimed to be out of the article she fancied, she had the bad taste to offer a bonus price. On Greenhaven, this is regarded as bribery, immorality, and economic subversion, to touch merely upon the highlights."

Smith sighed.

"Why will these young girls run around doing—"

"I don't believe you could call her a girl, exactly," Parrish interrupted.

"Well, this lady, then . . ."

"I wouldn't guarantee that either."

Smith shrugged and pursed his lips. "You'd be a better judge than I," he admitted innocently. "I yield to superior qualifications."

Lydman grinned. Parrish maintained his mask.

"I suppose that might make it even more dangerous for her," Smith went on. "I forget what you said the sentence was, but suppose she starts to get smart in jail. Would any snappy Terran humor pass there?"

"By no means!" said Parrish emphatically. "I would not expect them to burn her at the stake in this day and age, but they *would* talk about it as being one of the good old ways. Fortunately, their speaking and writing Terran makes this easy. Terrans are all black sinners, but plenty of Terrans are necessary around the spaceports. We keep a few agents among them. One of them is going to pull the paper trick to spring her."

"I'd rather leave them a bomb," said Lydman, almost to himself.

Smith frequently wondered that such a rugged man should speak in so quiet a voice. At times, Lydman used a monotone that was barely audible.

"We hope to destroy all evidence," added Parrish. "Otherwise, it will lead to the usual diplomatic notes, and the D.I.R. will be telling us we never were authorized to do any such thing."

"Yes," said Smith, nodding wearily. "Actually, you couldn't find our specific duties written down anywhere; and there is *nothing* we are forbidden to do either—as long as it succeeds. Well, none of us will see the day when the D.I.R. will publicly recognize us to the extent of chopping our heads into the basket. They *have* been yapping at me, though, for drawing complaints in the Gerson case."

Lydman had been sitting with his gaze narrowed upon a pencil gripped in his big fists. Now he raised his head, scenting interference in his own project.

"How can the Yoleenites complain? They claim they don't even have Gerson!"

"Easy!" Smith soothed him. "We have an embassy and spaceport there, remember, that you've been relying on. You had them make some inquiries, didn't you?"

"Had to confirm the report somehow. All we had was the story of a kidnapping from the captain of that freighter. It might not have been true."

"I realize that," said Smith.

"It wouldn't have been the first time a spacer got left behind because he didn't make countdown—or because they didn't want him around at payoff."

"Sure," Parrish agreed smoothly. "You could tell us about that."

Lydman turned to look at him, so suddenly that a silence fell among them. Parrish averted his gaze uncomfortably, and reached into the breast pocket of his maroon jacket for a box of cigarettes. He busied himself puffing one alight from the chemical lighter set in the bottom of the box.

One day I'll have to pull them apart, thought Smith, *and I'm not big enough. Where does my wife get the nerve to say the neighbors don't know what to make of an average guy like me, just because I can't talk about my work?*

"At any rate," he said quietly, "they took the attitude that even to ask them about the incident was insulting. It seemed to rock the top brass."

16

"What do *they* know about Yoleen?" growled Lydman, giving up his scrutiny of Parrish.

"Not a thing, probably. They make decisions on the basis of how many toes they've stubbed lately. Right now, it sounds like only routine panic. That reminds me—I meant to check with Emil Starke about that."

He shoved back his chair and stepped over to a phone table nearby. Switching on both screen and sound, he waited until the cute little blonde at the board came on.

"Pauline, get me Emil Starke at the D.I.R., please. Extension 1563."

"Yes, Mr. Smith," said Pauline, and disappeared from the screen.

In a few moments, Smith was greeting a man of about fifty, gray at the temples to the point of appearing over-distinguished.

"Listen, Emil," he said, getting down to business after the amenities about families and children had been observed. "I have a case on my hands concerning a planet named Yoleen—"

The man on the screen was already nodding.

"Yes, I heard they were chewing you about that this morning," he said, smiling. "I trust you preserved some sort of sang-froid?"

"What's in their minds?" asked Smith.

"Oh . . . it seems that the Space Force is nervous over the Yoleenites. They are unable to evaluate the culture comfortably. To cover themselves, I imagine, they send a warning now and then on the possibilities of hostile relations."

"Anything to it?"

Starke grimaced briefly.

"Unlikely. Some of the lads upstairs let it make them nervous."

Smith chuckled. "Upstairs," they came and went, but Starke and men like him ran things and knew what went on.

"Then I can go ahead without covering my tracks too deeply?" he asked. "I mean, I won't have to lie openly to my boss?"

"Give him a few days to see the other side," Starke assured him, "and he will be demanding to know why you have not taken steps. Have them taken by then!"

Smith thanked him for the advice, switched off, and returned to his place at the table. Nods from the others confirmed that they had heard.

"I have a feeling about those Yoleenites," grumbled Lydman.

Smith waited for elucidation, but the big man had sunk

into contemplation. The other two eyed him, then each other. Parrish shrugged ever so slightly. Smith gnawed at his lower lip.

"Well, then, you'll be going ahead with what you planned," he reminded Lydman.

"Oh, sure!" answered the ex-spacer, snapping out of it. "Can't help it. I've already sent him something useful."

The others smiled. "Something useful" was Lydman's term for a cleverly designed break-out instrument. Smith hoped that in this case it would not turn out to be a bomb.

"We dug a little mechanical crawler out of the files," Lydman went on. "The Yoleenites seem to build their cities like a conglomeration of pueblos, very intricate and with hardly any open streets. There would probably be a hundred routes in to Gerson, even if we knew exactly where he is. This gadget is adjusted to home on certain body temperatures which it can detect at some distance."

"And Gerson would be the only living thing there at ninety-eight point six."

"Exactly. Of course, the thing has a general direction and search pattern micro-taped in. That's the best they could do, because the boys have only a rough idea of where the cell would be."

"It sounds too easy to intercept," objected Parrish.

"That worries me a little," admitted Lydman. "It would be worse to fly something in, and it's impossible to send anyone in because they say they haven't got him. The gadget is set to have an affinity for dark corners, at least."

"And how does it get him out?" pursued Parrish.

"It carries a little pocket music player with micro-tapes that will actually play for a couple of hours. They can't tell for sure that Gerson didn't have it with him—if they spot it at all. When he opens the back as a little jingle in the first tune will instruct him to do, he has a miniature torch hot enough to cut the guts out of any lock between him and the outside."

"Someone will be watching for him, I suppose?" asked Smith.

"Sure. Once he's out of the place, the Yoleenites can hardly demand that we give back what they say they never had. Off to the embassy with him and onto the first ship! And I hope he kills a few of the bastards on the way out—they won't even have grounds for an official complaint!"

The other two avoided looking at him for a moment. Parrish stirred uneasily.

"I hope it—What I mean is, these Yoleenites give me an uneasy feeling the same as they do you, Bob. Experience

18

tells me that some of these hive-like cultures think along peculiar lines. No wonder the Space Force finds them hard to understand! I recommend that we open a general file on them."

"It might be just as well," Smith agreed, considering. "They may give us more business in the future."

He pushed back his chair and rose.

"Let's take a break while I see if any new reports have come in. Then maybe we can work out something on the new mess."

THREE

LOUIS TARANTO SAT ON HIS HEELS AGAINST THE baked clay wall of the cell, watching the sweat run down the face of his companion. Though he privately considered Harvey Meyers a very weak link, he had so far restrained himself from hinting as much. They were in this hole together, and he might well need the blubbery loudmouth's help to get out—if there were any way to get out.

Meyers sat on the single bench with which their jailers had provided them, staring mournfully at the rude table upon which he rested his elbows. He was unusually quiet, as if the heat had drained him of all anxiety.

Sloppy bum! thought Taranto. *He could at least comb his hair!*

They were allowed occasional access to toilet articles which the Syssokans had obtained from the one Terran officially in residence on the planet. Taranto had shaved the day before, but the other had not bothered for more than a week. Meyers was perhaps an inch short of six feet and must weigh two hundred pounds Terran. He had a loose mouth between pudgy cheeks. His little blue eyes seemed always to be prying except during periods such as the present when he was feeling sorry for himself. He had been a medic in the same spaceship in which Taranto had been a ventilation mechanic.

"Glad I was never sick," Taranto muttered to himself.

Meyers looked up.

"Huh?"

"I said I'm glad I was never sick," repeated Taranto deliberately, thinking, *Let him figure that out if he can!*

19

"This heat's enough to make anybody sick," complained Meyers. "Why do they have to keep us up on the top floor of the tower, anyway?"

"You expect a luxury suite in the cellar? What kind of jail were you ever in where the prisoners got the best?"

"Who says I was ever in jail?" demanded Meyers defensively.

Taranto grinned slightly, but made no reply. After a moment, the other returned to his study of the table. He breathed in loudly, his shoulders heaving as if he had been running. To avoid the sight, Taranto let his eyes wander for the thousandth time around the walls of the square cell.

The large blocks of baked clay were turning from dun to gray in the twilight seeping through the four small window openings. Overhead, they curved together to form a high arch that was the peak of the tower. Besides table and bench, the room contained a clay water jug a yard high, a wooden bucket, a battered copper cooking pot, and a pile of coarse straw upon which lay the two gray shirts the spacers had discarded in the heat. In the center of the floor was a wooden trap door which Taranto eyed speculatively.

He reminded himself that he must suppress his longing to smash the next Syssokan head that appeared in the opening.

"It's getting near time," he remarked after a few minutes.

Meyers peered at the patches of sky revealed by the windows. They were losing the glare of Syssokan daylight. There had been a wisp or two of cloud earlier, but these had either blown over or faded into the deepening gray of the sky.

"Listen at the door!" ordered Taranto, impatient at having to remind the other.

He rose, wiped perspiration from his face with the palms of both hands, and rubbed them in turn on the thighs of his gray pants. He was inches shorter than Meyers, and twenty pounds or more lighter, but his bare shoulders bulged powerfully. A little fat softened the lines of his belly without concealing the existence of an underlying layer of solid muscle. He moved with a heavy, padding gait, like a large carnivore whose natural grace is revealed only at top speed.

Meyers watched him resentfully.

Why couldn't I have made it to one of the other emergency rockets? he asked himself. *Imagine a bunch of crazy savages that say even landing here is a crime!*

He supposed that Taranto would have pointed to the sizable city where they were held if he had heard the Syssokans called savages. Meyers thought the trouble with Taranto was that he was too physical, too much of a dumb flunky who spoiled Meyers' efforts to talk them out of trouble.

I had a better break coming, he thought.

He wished he had been in a rocket with one of the ship's officers who might have known about Syssoka. They would have gone into an orbit about the planet's star and put out a call for help to the nearest Terran base or ship. As it was, they might be given up for lost even if the other rockets were picked up. The course they had been on before the explosion had been designed to pass this system by a good margin.

Taranto, he recalled, had thought them lucky to have picked up the planet on the little escape ship's instruments. Taranto, decided Meyers, thought he was a hot pilot because he had been a few years in space. He had not looked so good bending the rocket across that ridge of rock out in the desert. They should have taken a chance on coming down in the city here.

They had just about straightened themselves out after that landing when they had seen the party of Syssokans on the way. It had not taken them long to reach the wreck. They could even speak Terran, and no pidgin-Terran either. Then it turned out that they did not like spacers of any race landing without permission. There had been a war with the next star system; and the laws now said there should be only one alien of any race permitted to reside on Syssoka except for brief visits by licensed spaceships.

"What's the matter with our government?" muttered Meyers.

"What?" asked Taranto, turning from one of the windows.

"I said what's the matter with the Terran Government? Why don't they pitch a couple of bombs down here, an' show these skinny nuts who's running the galaxy? Who are they to call *us* aliens?"

Taranto turned again to the eighteen inch square window, set like the other three in the center of its wall at the level of his shoulders.

"They're posting their sentries on the city wall for the night," he told Meyers. "The thing should be flying in here any time now."

"*If* it comes," said Meyers grumpily. "Something will go wrong with that too."

The other spat out the window that faced the main part of the Syssokan city, then padded to the one opposite. Strange patterns of stars gleamed already in the sky over the desert.

21

The air that blew against his damp face was a trifle cooler.

Should I tell the slob about that? he wondered. *Naw—he'd try to breathe it all! Let him sweat, as long as he listens for the Syssokans!*

Meyers had left his bench to crouch over the trap door. There was no reason to expect their jailers, but the Syssokans had a habit of popping up at odd times. The evening meal was usually brought well after dark, however.

"Do you think it will really get here again?" asked Meyers. "What if they spot it?"

Taranto grunted. He was watching something he thought was one of the flying insects that thickened the Syssokan twilight. Seconds later, he ducked away from the window as a pencil-sized thing with two pairs of flailing wings darted through the opening.

It whirled about the dim cell. Meyers flapped his hands about his head. The third time around, the insect passed within Taranto's reach; and he batted it out of the air with a feline sweep of his left hand. It fell against the base of the wall and twitched for a few minutes.

Meyers squinted at him, examining the slightly flattened nose and the meaty cheeks that gave Taranto a deceptively plump look.

"You're quick, all right," he admitted. "They used to say in the ship that you were a boxer. What made you a spacer?"

"Too short," said Taranto laconically. "Five-eight, an' I grew into a light-heavy."

"What did that have to do with it?"

"I did all right for a while. When I could get in on them, they'd go down an' stay down. Then they learned to stick an' run on me. It was either grow a longer arm or quit."

"Maybe you should have quit sooner," said Meyers, for no good reason except that he resented Taranto and blamed him for their predicament.

"Why should I?" asked Taranto, with a cold stare. "It was good money. Even after having my eyebrows fixed, I got a nice nest-egg back on Terra. Nothing really shows on me except the habit of a short haircut."

Meyers ran his fingers through his own unkempt hair.

"What was that for?" he asked.

"Oh . . . it don't wave in the air so much when you stop a jab. Looks better, to the judges."

Meyers grunted. *He'd like to believe it doesn't show on him!* he thought.

Suddenly, he bent down to place an ear against the trap door. A petulant grimace twisted his features.

"They're on the ladder," he whispered. "Wouldn't you know?"

He straightened up and walked softly back to his bench. Taranto remained at the window. It was a perfectly natural place for him to be, he decided.

A few moments later, the trap door creaked up, letting yellow light burst into the cell. It came from a clumsy electric lantern in the grip of the first Syssokan who climbed into the chamber. Two others followed, suggestively fingering pistols that would have been considered crude on Terra two centuries earlier.

The individual with the light was typical of his race, a tall, cadaverous humanoid with pale, greenish-gray skin made up of tiny scales. His nose was flatter than that of a Terran ape, and his chin consisted mostly of a hanging fold of scaly skin. His ears were set very low on a narrow, pointed skull. Occasionally, they made small motions as if to fold in upon themselves.

The Syssokans were clad in garments not unlike loose, sleeveless pajamas, over which they wore leather harness for their weapons. The leader's suit was red, but the other two wore a dull brown.

"Iss all ssatissfactory?" asked the one in charge, staring about the cell with large, black eyes.

"All right," said Taranto stonily.

He thought that a Syssokan would never have answered that way. They were vain of their extraordinary linguistic ability, and commonly spoke three or four alien tongues. Only an unfortunate inability to control excessive sibilance marred their Terran. Taranto felt like wiping his face, but realized that it was only sweat.

The Syssokan prowled around the room, examining each of the simple furnishings with a flickering glance. He took note of the food left in the copper pot. He checked the level of water in the big jar. He found the dead insect, which he sniffed and slipped into a pouch at his belt. When he passed Taranto, the latter eyed him in measuring fashion.

The Syssokan halted out of reach.

"You have been warned to obey all orderss here," he said, staring between the two Terrans.

"What's the trouble now?" demanded Meyers when it became apparent that the poker-faced Taranto intended to say nothing.

"There wass a quesstion by the Terran we allow on the world. How can he know of your complaints? He was told only of your ssentence."

'We told you there would be protests from our govern-

23

ment," said Meyers. "All we did was land on your planet in an emergency: We're only too willing to leave. You have no right to keep us locked up in these conditions."

"It iss a violation of our law," said the Syssokan imperturbably. "You go automatically to jail. We permit only one of every sky people to live here. Who could tell yours that you complain of thiss place?"

"Listen, you better be careful of us Terrans!" blustered Meyers. "We have ways—"

"Shut up!" said Taranto without raising his voice.

He had inched forward, but stopped now as the two guards at the trap door gave him their attention.

The Syssokan with the lantern also turned to him. Taranto looked over the latter's shoulder. The window was black; the twilight of Syssoka was brief.

Meyers had flushed and was scowling at him with outthrust lower lip, but Taranto's icy order had spilled the wind from his sails.

"Perhapss you have had too much water," suggested the Syssokan, regarding Taranto with interest. "If you have done ssomething, it iss besst to tell me."

Taranto returned the stare. He wondered why all the Syssokans he had seen, though rather fragile in build, were relatively thick-waisted. They looked to him as if a couple of solid hooks to the body would find a soft target.

It was unlikely that the Syssokan could read the facial expression of an alien Terran. It was probably some tenseness in Taranto's stance that caused the native to step back.

The Terran strained his ears to pick up any unusual noise outside the window during the pause. He heard nothing except the whir of night insects.

Their jailer paced once more around the cell, and Taranto cursed himself for arousing suspicion. Perhaps, he hoped, it was only annoyance.

But what could I do? he asked himself. *Let Meyers spill it?*

In the end, with Taranto answering in monosyllables and Meyers intimidated into an unnatural reserve, the Syssokans retired. The darkness closed in upon the Terrans as they listened to the creaking of the ladder below the trap door.

"Give them time," advised Taranto, hearing Meyers move toward the exit.

They waited in the silent dark until Meyers could stand it no longer.

"They won't come back," he whispered.

"Well, make sure," said Taranto shortly. "Get your ear to the wood!"

He felt his way to the window that faced away from the

24

city. After the heat of the day, the air blowing in was almost cold; and he considered putting on his shirt. The realization that he would have to scrabble around the pile of straw for it gave him pause. His next thought was that he might come up with the wrong shirt, and that discouraged him completely.

His eyes had adjusted enough to the night to pick out the low hills of the desert where they broke the line of the horizon. Starlight glinted softly where there were stretches of sand. He settled down to wait, his arms folded upon the ledge of the window.

It was nearly half an hour later, when he suspected Meyers of dozing on the trap door, that Taranto heard something more than an insect zip past the window. He backed away and hissed to attract Meyers' attention.

"Did it come?" whispered the other.

"I think so," answered Taranto.

A tiny hum drifted through the window. Into the opening, timidly, edged a small, hovering shape.

"Okay," said Taranto in a low voice, even though he knew the room was being scanned by an infra-red detector.

The shape blossomed out with a midget light. Enough of the glow was reflected from the adobe walls to reveal that a miniature flying mechanism the size of a man's hand had landed on the window ledge. After a moment, its rotors ceased their whirring. Taranto jabbed backward with an elbow as he heard Meyers creep up behind him.

"Listen at the door, dammit!" he snarled. "All we need is to get caught at this, an' we'll be here till they turn out the sun!"

"Taranto!" piped a tiny voice from the machine. "Are you ready, Taranto?"

"Go ahead!"

"Two pills coming out of the hold." The voice was clear enough in the stillness of the Syssokan night.

A hatch in the belly of the little flyer slid back. Two capsules spilled out on the window ledge. Taranto scooped them up.

"You each take one, with water," instructed the voice. "Better wait till just before dawn. You told me they bring your food an hour later."

"That's right," whispered Taranto.

"That will give the stuff time to act. For all they can tell, you will both be deader than a burned-out meteorite."

"Then what?"

"So they will follow their normal custom with the dead—

take you out to the desert to mummify. This thing will hover overhead to spot the location."

"Do they just . . . leave us?"

"Yes, as far as anybody has ever been able to find out. I talked to the Capellan next door in the foreign quarter here, and he says they might not leave you in one of their own burial grounds. Otherwise, I would hate to take the chance of having this gadget seen in the daylight."

"All right, so we're out in the desert," said Taranto. "How does this ship you arranged for pick us up? We'll still be out for the count."

"I plan to tell them where to touch down. I can talk louder by radio, you know, that I can to you now. They will grab your 'bodies' and scramble for space. Against the sunset, they may not even be seen from the city. If they are, I never heard of them."

"Who are they?" asked Taranto.

"Some bunch hired for the job by the D.I.R.'s Department 99. Just as well not to ask where they come from or what their usual line is."

"I ain't got any questions at all, if they get us out of here," said Taranto.

He watched as the hatch closed itself and the tiny light blinked out. The rotors began to spin, and two minutes later they were alone.

"Come and get yours," said the spacer.

He reached out with his empty hand to guide Meyers to him, then very carefully delivered one of the capsules to the other.

"We're supposed to swallow that big lump?" whispered Meyers.

"Just don't lose it," admonished Taranto.

He relayed the instructions as precisely as he could.

"One thing more," he concluded. "You stay awake to make sure I stay awake until it's time to take the stuff."

"We could take watches," suggested Meyers.

"I could," said Taranto bluntly, "but I'm not sure about you. In the second place, I ain't going to have you sleep while I don't. We're going to play this as safe as possible."

Meyers grumbled something inaudibly. In the darkness, a sardonic smile twisted Taranto's lips.

"If you know how," he advised, "pray! We're goin' to our funeral in the morning."

FOUR

WESTERVELT SAT AT HIS LITTLE DESK IN THE
corner, doodling out possible ways and means of breaking
out of a cell thirty fathoms or so under water. From time
to time Beryl or Simonetta offered a suggestion. He knew
that everyone in the office was probably engaged in the same
puzzle. Smith believed in general brain-storming in getting
a project started, since no one could tell where a good idea
might not originate.

"If I ever get into space," Willie muttered, "it will never
be to a planet as wet as Trident. What ever made this Harris
think he was a pearl diver?"

"Is that what he was after?" asked Beryl.

"No, I just made that up."

He glanced over at Simonetta, who winked and continued
with the letter she was transcribing. An earphone reproduced
Smith's dictation from his tape. As she listened, she edited
mentally and spoke into the microphone of her typing machine, which transcribed her words as type. Westervelt realized that it was more difficult than it seemed to do the job so
smoothly. He had noticed Beryl rewriting letters two or
three times, and Parrish was more likely than the boss to
set down his thoughts in a logical order.

"I've heard so many wild ideas in this office," said Beryl,
"that I simply don't know where to start. How do they
decide on a good way?"

"They guess, just the way we've been doing. They're bet-
er guessers than we are, from experience."

"It's just a matter of judgment, I suppose," Beryl admitted.

"They make their share of mistakes," Simonetta put in.

"Yeah, I read an old report on a great one," said Westervelt. "Ever hear of the time they were shipping oxygen
tanks to three spacers jailed out around Mizar?"

Simonetta stopped talking her letter, and the girls gave
Willie their attention.

"It seems," he continued, "that an exploring ship landed
on a planet of that star and found a kind of civilization
they hadn't bargained for. The natives breathed air with a
high chlorine content; so when they grabbed three of the

27

crew for hostages, the ship had to keep supplying fresh tanks of oxygen."

"How long could they keep that up?" asked Beryl.

"Not indefinitely, anyway. They weren't recovering any carbon dioxide for processing, the way they would in the ship. The captain figured he'd better lift and orbit while he tried to negotiate. Meanwhile, he sent to the Department for help, and they came up with a poor guess."

"What?"

"They got the captain to disguise some spacesuit rockets as oyxgen tanks and send them down by the auxiliary rocket they were using to make deliveries and keep contact. The idea was that the prisoners would fly themselves over the walls like angels, the rocket would snatch them up, and they'd all filter the green-white light of Mizar from their lenses forever."

"And why didn't it work?"

"Oh, it worked," said Westervelt. "It worked beautifully. The only trouble was that when they got these three guys aboard and were picking up stellar speed, they found that the Mizarians had pulled a little sleight of hand. They'd stuck three of their own into the Terran spacesuits—pretty cramped, but able to move—and sent them to spy out the ship. Well, the captain took one look and realized it was all over. He couldn't supply the Mizarians with enough chlorine to keep them alive until they could be sent back. He just kept going."

"But the men they left behind!" exclaimed Beryl. "What happened to them?"

Westervelt shrugged.

"They never exactly found out."

Beryl, horrified, turned to Simonetta, who stared reflectively at the wall.

"For all we know," said the dark girl, "they were dead already."

"It was about even," said Westervelt. "The Mizarians never heard exactly what happened to theirs either."

There was a period of silence while they considered that angle. Simonetta finally said, "Why don't you tell her about the time they gave that spacer the hormone treatment for a disguise?"

"Oh . . . you tell it," said Westervelt, trapped. "You know it better than I do."

"That one," began Simonetta, "happened on a world where there's a colony from Terra that isn't much talked about. It's a sort of Amazon culture, and they don't allow men. They were set to execute this fellow who smuggled himself in for

28

ı lark, when the Department started shipping him drugs that changed his appearance."

Westervelt admired Beryl's wide-eyed intentness.

"Finally," Simonetta continued, "his appearance changed so much that he could dress up and pass for a woman anywhere. He just walked out when the next scheduled spaceship landed, and was halfway back to Terra before they finished searching the woods for him. It made trouble, though."

"What happened?" breathed Beryl.

"They never quite succeeded in changing him back. His wife wound up divorcing him for infidelity when he gave birth to twins."

Beryl straightened up abruptly.

"Oh . . . ! You—come on, now!"

Westervelt reminded himself that the blush must have resulted less from the joke than from having been taken in. They were still laughing when a buzzer sounded at Beryl's desk phone. She flipped the switch, listened for a moment, then rose with a toss of her blonde head at Westervelt.

"Mr. Parrish wants me to help him research in the dead files," she said. "I bet *he* won't try that kind of gag on me!"

"No," muttered Westervelt as she strode out, "he has some all his own."

He looked up to find Simonetta watching him with a grin. She shook her head ruefully as Westervelt grew a flush to match Beryl's.

"Willie, Willie!" she said sadly. "You aren't letting that bottle blonde bother you? I didn't think you were that kind of boy!"

Westervelt grinned back, at some cost.

"Is there another kind?" he asked. "After all, Si, she's only been around a few weeks. It's the novelty. I'll get used to her."

"*Sure* you will," said Simonetta.

She returned to her letters, and Westervelt hunched over his desk to brood. He wondered what Parrish and Beryl were up to in the file room. He could think of no innocent reason to wander in on business of his own. Perhaps, he reflected, he did not really want to; he might overhear something he would regret.

He passed some time without directing a single thought to the problems of the Department. Then the door beyond Simonetta opened and Smith strolled out. He carried a pad as if he, too, had been doodling.

"Well, Willie," he said cheerfully, "what are we going to do about this Harris fellow?"

29

"All I can think of, Mr. Smith, is to offer to trade them a few people we could do without," said Westervelt.

Smith grinned. He seemed to be willing to make up a little list.

"Some who never would be missed, eh? And let's head the page with people who take messages from thinking fish!"

He pottered about for a few moments before winding up seated on a corner of the unoccupied secretarial desk.

"I was actually thinking of skin divers," he confided. "Then I realized that if it takes a twenty foot monster to wander the undersea wilds of Trident without being intimidated, maybe those waters wouldn't be too safe for Terran swimmers."

"Unless they could get one of the monsters for a guide," suggested Westervelt.

The three of them pondered that possibility.

"I can see it now," said Simonetta. "My name Swishy. Me good guide. You want find pearl? Not allowed here; we no steal from other fish!"

They laughed, and Smith demanded to know how one *thought* in pidgin talk. They discussed the probability of fraud in the reports that Smith had received, and concluded reluctantly that, whether or not some trick might be involved, there was bound to be some truth in the story.

"I suppose we'll have to use this fishy network to locate him," sighed Smith at last. "It would take too long to ship out parts of a small sub to be assembled on Trident. The whole thing makes me wonder if I'll ever eat another seafood dinner!"

"Maybe somebody else will think of something," said Westervelt, partly to conceal the fact that he himself had come up with nothing.

"Tell you what," said Smith, nodding. "Suppose you go along and see how Bob Lydman is making out, while I sign these letters. You might check at the com room sometime, too, in case anything else on the case comes in."

Westervelt agreed, made sure he had something in his pocket to write upon should the need arise, and left.

A few minutes later, he reached the end of the corridor, having cocked an ear at the door of the old file office as he passed and heard Beryl giggling at some remark by Parrish. He unclenched his teeth and knocked on Lydman's door.

He waited a minute and tried again, but there was still no answer.

He hesitated, wondering what would happen should he walk in and find that Lydman was physically present but not in a mood to recognize any one else's existence. Slowly, he walked back to the washroom on the opposite side of the hall.

Washing his hands with deliberation, Westervelt decided that it might be best to get Lydman on the phone. He could not, in fact, understand why inside phone calls were not more popular in the office. He supposed that the face-to-face habit had grown up among the staff, probably reflecting Smith's preference for getting everyone personally involved in everything. There might even be a deeper cause—they were so often in contact with distant places by the tenuous beaming of interstellar signals that there must be a certain reassurance and sense of security in having within physical reach the person to whom one was speaking.

"I'll have to watch for that if I stay here long enough," Westervelt told himself. "You don't have to be a prizefighter to get punchy, I guess."

He examined himself critically in the mirror over the sink, thinking that he could do with a neater appearance. A coin in the slot of a dispenser on the wall bought him a disposable paper comb with which he smoothed down his dark hair.

I need a haircut almost as bad as Castor P. he thought. I wonder if that really stands for Pollux? What a thing for parents to do! On the other hand, from people that came up with one like him, you'd expect almost anything!

No one came in while he was in the washroom, much as he would have welcomed an excuse for conversation. He dawdled his way through the door into the corridor, not liking the thought of inflicting his presence upon Beryl and Parrish. That meant he would have to walk back as far as the spare conference room to find a phone.

"Of course, there's the lab," he muttered.

That was only a few steps away, and he could hardly do much damage between the door and the phone.

Reaching the end of the corridor once more, he decided to make one last try at Lydman's door. Again, there was no reply to his knock, so he turned away to the laboratory door and entered.

He was faced by a vista of tables, workbenches with power tools, and diverse assemblies of testing apparatus, most of the latter dusty and presenting the appearance of gold-bergs knocked together for temporary use and then shoved aside until someone might need a part from one of them. By far the greater space, however, was occupied by shelves and crates and stacks of small cartons or loosely wrapped packages in which various gadgets seemed to be stored after plans of them had been transmitted to the field. Half a dozen large files for drawings and blueprints reached nearly to the ceiling. Racks of instruments in relatively recent use or consideration stood here and there among the tables and workbenches.

To Westervelt's right, near the far wall behind which lay the communications room, he caught sight of a prowling figure. He recognized Lydman's broad shoulders and hesitated.

The ex-spacer had paused to examine a gadget lying on one of the tables. From Westervelt's position, it appeared to be a wristwatch or something similar. Lydman picked it up and turned toward a part of the wall where a thick steel plate had been fastened to an insulated partition of brick. He raised the "watch" to eye level, as if aiming.

A thin pencil of white flame leaped from the instrument to spatter sparks against the already scarred and stained steel. Sucked up by the air-conditioning, the small puff of smoke disappeared so quickly that Westervelt realized that the scorched odor was entirely in his imagination.

Lydman replaced the instrument casually before strolling over to another table. He inspected an open pack of cigarettes with a grim smile, but let them lie there in plain sight. Westervelt reminded himself never to grub one of those, just on general principles. Lydman went on to a small cylinder somewhat larger than an old-fashioned battery flashlight. Something clicked under his finger, and from one end of the cylinder emerged the folding blades of a portable fan. The ex-spacer pressed a second switch position to start them spinning. He turned the fan to blow across his face, as if to check its cooling power, then held the thing at arm's length as he thumbed the switch to a third position.

A low, humming sound reached Westervelt. It rose rapidly in pitch until it passed beyond his hearing range. He shook his head slightly. For some reason, he found it difficult to concentrate. Perhaps Lydman's presence, unexpected as it was, had upset him, he thought. He decided that he must be getting a dizzy spell of some sort. Then he became concerned lest he turn nauseous.

The final stage, hardly a minute after Lydman had last moved the switch, found Westervelt tensing as a wave of sheer panic swept over him.

He stepped back toward the door, noticing dizzily that Lydman wore a strange expression too. Part of the youth's mind wondered if some of the ultra-sonic effect were reflected from the walls to the ex-spacer; another part insisted upon leaving the scene as hastily as possible.

32

He got himself into the corridor again, actually panting as he eased the door closed behind him. He started to walk, finding his knees a trifle loose. Passing the washroom, he hesitated; but he decided that he could make it to the conference room. Once there, however, he slipped inside and sat down to recover.

"What does it take to have a mind like that?" he whispered to himself. "It's like a hobby to him. I think some day I ought to look for a job with reasonably normal people!"

A few minutes of peace and quiet refreshed him. He returned to the main office, just as Smith was surrendering a stack of signed letters to Simonetta Diorio. They looked around as he entered.

"Well, Willie, did he have anything going?" asked Smith.

"I ... uh ... he was kind of busy," said Westervelt.

"What did he seem to have in mind?" Smith started to reach for Simonetta's phone switch.

"He . . . that is . . . I didn't ask him. He was . . . busy, in the lab."

"Oh," said Smith.

He peered at Westervelt's expression, and added, "Then ... perhaps we'd better not disturb him. It might spoil any ideas he's putting together."

Westervelt managed a grunt of assent as he turned to walk back to his desk.

Whatever he's putting together, he thought, *I'd rather stay out of the way.*

He hunched over his desk, staring unseeingly at the notes he had scribbled earlier. He was vaguely conscious of the cessation of talk in the background, but he did not notice Simonetta's approach until the girl stood beside him.

"What happened, Willie?" she asked. "You look as if he threw you out."

"No. Not deliberately, anyhow," said Westervelt. "At least, I don't *think* he knew I was even there—although how can you tell if he doesn't want to let on?"

He told her what had happened in the laboratory. She nodded thoughtfully.

"I suppose it has its uses," said Westervelt. "I hate to think of the way he plays around with things in there. Wasn't there a time when someone killed himself in that lab?"

"That was years ago," said Simonetta.

She hugged herself as if feeling a sudden chill, her large, soft eyes serious. Westervelt realized that she was actually a very beautiful girl, much more so than Beryl, and he wondered why he felt so differently about them. Simonetta

33

seemed too nice to fit the ideas he got concerning Beryl. Something told him that his thinking was mixed up.

I guess you just grow out of that, he reflected silently. *Maybe they're the same under the skin.*

FIVE

WHEN BERYL WALKED IN, WESTERVELT WAS AT one of the tall windows with Simonetta, dialing filter combinations to make the most of the setting sun. They had the edge of it showing as a deep crimson ball beside another building in the vicinity.

"What are you two doping out?" asked the blonde. "Some disappearing trick?"

Simonetta laughed as Westervelt shoved the dial setting to afternoon normal.

"It's an idea," he said, scowling at Beryl.

"For underwater?" she demanded mockingly.

"Ever hear of a squid?" retorted Westervelt. "*They* hide themselves underwater. Maybe a cloud of dye would be as good as a filter."

"Willie, that *is* an idea!" said Simonetta. "You ought to tell Mr. Smith."

Westervelt looked at her sourly. Now Beryl knew that they really had been wasting time, and had a point to score against him in their next exchange.

Oh, well. I can't hold a thing like that against Si, he thought. *I can think of people who'd be on the way to Smitty already, calling it their own idea.*

Beryl had done a ladylike collapse into her chair and crossed her legs. She dug into her purse for cigarettes and requested a light.

"Why don't you buy a brand with a lighter in the box?" asked Westervelt.

Nevertheless, he walked over to the switchboard cubicle for the office desk lighter that had been appropriated by Pauline. Returning with it after a moment, he lit Beryl's cigarette and inquired, "Well, what did you and Parrish dig up?"

"I don't know," she sighed, leaning back, "but, boy, did we dig!"

34

"Yeah, I thought I heard the shovel clink once," said Westervelt, thinking of the laughter he had heard through the door of the dead file office.

Beryl, concerned with her own complaints, ignored him.

"We must have looked up thirty or forty cases," she went on. "I never even heard of most of those places on the newscasts!"

"Did he find anything that gave him an idea?" asked Simonetta.

"Not a thing! There seemed to be some real crazy spots in the records, but nobody ever got in jail at the bottom of an ocean."

"You'd think it would have happened sometime," said Simonetta thoughtfully.

"I suppose," suggested Westervelt, "that on any planet where Terrans were taken underwater, they didn't live long enough to be one of our cases. On a place like Trident, they usually wouldn't have any trouble. They'd stay on land, and any local life would stay in the sea. It took a nut like Harris to go poking around where he wasn't wanted."

"That's what Mr. Parrish hinted," said Beryl. "All I know is that it sounds like a story out of a laughing academy. They shouldn't allow them to get into places like that."

"Then we'd all be looking for work," said Westervelt. "Don't complain, Beryl—maybe it will happen to you someday."

The blonde shivered and turned to face her desk.

"Not me," she declared. "I'm staying on Terra, even if they do offer me a field trip as a sort of vacation."

Ah, he's already started that line on her, thought Westervelt. *I wonder if there's anything in the files on how to spring a secretary from a penthouse?*

Lydman and Parrish walked in, the latter pausing to exchange remarks with Pauline, the switchboard operator. A moment later, Smith opened his door as if expecting someone. He must have phoned them for a change, Westervelt realized.

"Oh, there you are, Willie," said the chief. "I suppose you might as well sit in on this too. We might need something, and meanwhile, you can be picking up a tip or two."

Westervelt rose and followed the others into Smith's office, where he took a chair by the window. The others clustered around the chief's desk, a vast plateau of silvery plastic strewn with a hodge-podge of papers and tapes.

The office itself was like a small museum. The walls were lined with photographs, mostly of poor quality but showing "interesting" devices that had been used in various department cases. The ones in which the color was better usually

35

showed Smith in company with two or three men wearing space uniforms and self-conscious looks. Sometimes, a more assured individual was shown in the act of presenting some sort of memento or letter of appreciation to Smith. Lydman and Parrish also appeared in several of the pictures.

The record of our best cases, thought Westervelt. *The bad ones are buried in the files.*

Standing along the walls, or on little tables and bases of their own, were a good many models of spaceships, planetary systems, and non-humanoid beings. A few of the latter statues were enough to have made Beryl declare she was perfectly happy to stay out of Smith's office and be someone else's secretary. One model, which Westervelt secretly longed to examine at leisure, showed an entire city with its surrounding landscape on a distant planet.

Westervelt tore his attention from the mementoes and turned toward the group as Smith settled himself behind the desk.

"This is no longer even approximately funny," said the department head. "I've had a few calls put through. Do you know how little we're going to have to work with?"

"I gather that it is not very much," said Parrish calmly.

"There are less than fifty Terrans on that whole planet!" declared Smith, running the fingers of one hand through his already untidy hair. "The nearest colony or friendly space-port from which we could have equipment sent in is twenty odd lightyears away."

"Well, that could be done," said Lydman mildly.

"Oh, of course, it could be done," admitted Smith. "But how long do we have to fool around? We don't know under what conditions Harris is being held."

Parrish leaned forward to rest his elbows on Smith's desk.

"We can deduce some of them pretty well," he suggested. "In the first place, if he got out several messages—which we'll have to assume he did—they must have found some means of providing him with air."

"He could have lived a while on the air in this submarine he built," said Lydman.

"Yes, but in that case, he would have used its radio for communication. We have to assume that they pried him out somehow, no?"

The others nodded.

"He wouldn't last too long in a spacesuit, even if they pumped in air under pressure," said Lydman judiciously.

"So they must have built some kind of structure to house him, if only a big tank," said Parrish.

Westervelt stirred, then closed his mouth rather than inter-

36

rupt. Smith, however, had seen the motion and looked up.

"Speak up, Willie," he invited. "It won't sound any sillier than anything else that's been said in this room." .

"I . . . I was wondering about these Tridentians," said Westervelt. "Does anybody know how they live? Do they have cities built on the sea bottom?"

"If they have water jet vehicles, they certainly have the technical—"

Smith stopped as he saw Parrish lean back and roll his eyes toward the ceiling.

"What now, Pete?" he demanded apprehensively.

"I don't know why that didn't occur to me sooner," groaned Parrish. "A hundred to one they have a nomadic set-up. It would be typical, with an environment like that. This is worse than we thought."

"You mean," muttered Smith after a few moments of silence, "how can we get a direction fix on a thought?"

"Something like that," said Parrish. "I suppose they have bases, where they keep permanent manufacturing facilities. Probably set up at points where they have access to minerals—unless they know how to extract what they need from the water itself."

"Nothing hard about that," agreed Smith. "I'll have to send out a few more questions. Of course, they'll take the attitude that I should be doing something instead of asking about irrelevant subjects . . ."

"We're used to that," smiled Parrish, showing his beautiful teeth.

Westervelt wondered how broadly he would smile if it were his own responsibility. He had an idea that Parrish might be rather less than half as charming if he were running the operation and not getting much help from the others in solving the problem. He had to admit, however, that the man had a knack for spotting alien culture patterns. When he had asked his question about the cities, it was merely because he had half-pictured some Terran-style dome underwater and knew that that image was unlikely.

"Anyway," Parrish was going on, "we should probably think of them as being free as birds to go where they like. Even before they developed machines, they probably migrated about their world by swimming. I gather that these other . . . fish, I suppose we'll have to call them . . ."

"Thinking fish!" murmured Smith sadly. He ran his hand through his hair again.

"I suppose those things still do, besides other types we still haven't heard of, which would fill the place of Terran animals. So, then—we'll have to look for temporary loca-

37

tions and think in terms of a fast raid rather than a careful penetration."

"If we could find them, there must be some way we could armor a few spacesuits against pressure and drop down on them," said Lydman. "I think I can dig up a weapon or two that will work underwater in a way these clams never thought of."

"Maybe we could do better to have Swishy the thinking fish hypnotize them into bringing Harris back," said Westervelt.

They looked at him thoughtfully, and he was horrified to see his joke being taken seriously. He squirmed in his chair by the window, wishing he had kept his mouth shut.

"I wonder . . ." mused Smith. "If they can actually exchange thoughts. . . ."

"They might have natural defenses," said Parrish tentatively.

"What could we bribe a fish with?" asked Lydman, but hopefully rather than derisively.

Smith made another note, then drummed his fingers on his desk top. The four of them sat in silence. Westervelt hoped that the others were engaged in more productive thoughts than his own. It was nice to have their attention, and get the reputation of a bright young man who came up with suggestions; but when they decided upon some reasonable course of action they might remember him for making a foolish remark.

"Willie," said Smith, coming to a decision, "circulate around and ask the others if they can stick it out a couple of hours tonight. Maybe there's time to pry some useful information out of Trident, and at least get something started before we close down. If I know some guy out in space is working on it, I can sleep anyway."

Westervelt left his place by the window and went into the outer office. He told Simonetta and Beryl. The latter acted less than thrilled. Westervelt wondered jealously what kind of date she had scheduled for the evening. He stopped at the window of the switchboard cubbyhole.

"Oh, it's you, Willie!" exclaimed Pauline.

"Yeah, you can turn on the projector again," he grinned. "What is it, a love movie?"

Pauline edged a small tape projector out from behind the side of her board.

"It's homework, if you have to know," she told him.

"That's right, you still go to college," Westervelt recalled. "Why don't you switch to alien psychology? Then you could qualify for office manager around here."

"When do we have alien visitors here? Once in a ringed moon!"

"Who is to say which are the aliens?" said Westervelt. "There are days when I think I could feel more understanding to something with twelve tentacles and a tank of chlorine than to a lot of the mentalities that get loose right in this office. There's a crash program on for the evening, by the way, and Smitty wants the staff to hang on a while."

A look of dismay flashed over Pauline's youthful features.

"I know; you have a class tonight," Westervelt deduced. "Chuck it all. Stay in the file room with Mr. Parrish and you'll learn twice as much."

Pauline offered to throw the projector at him, but laughed. Westervelt told her that no one would miss her if she connected a few of the main office phones to outside lines and hooked up the communications room with Smith's desk.

He left her wondering if she ought to stay anyhow, and headed for the hall. Halfway along to the communications room, he heard the elevator doors open and close. He stopped and looked back.

Around the corner strolled one of the TV men, Joe Rosenkrantz. Westervelt looked at his watch and realized that it was a shift change for the communications personnel, who kept touch with the universe twenty-four hours a day.

In case someone somewhere makes a dumb mistake like Harris, thought Westervelt. *They overdo it a little, I think. I suppose it's the typical pride and joy of Terran technical culture to signal halfway across the galaxy to fix something that might have been cured beforehand when Harris was a little boy. I wonder what the psychologists should have done about me to keep me out of a place like this?*

"Hello, Willie," said Rosenkrantz, catching up. "Going to the com room?"

Westervelt admitted as much, and gave the operator a brief outline of the afternoon's developments. Rosenkrantz remained unperturbed.

"Hope they don't get intoxicated with ingenuity, and insist on sending messages all over," he grunted. "I was looking forward to a quiet night shift."

They went in to tell Colborn, who took it well. He pointed out to Westervelt that he would in no case have been concerned with the overtime operation. When he was relieved, he was relieved—period.

"I forget this crazy place the minute the elevator door closes behind me," he said grinning, having handed over to Rosenkrantz his log and a few unofficial comments about traffic he had heard during recent hours. "There are some who wait till they hit the street, but I believe in a clean cut. I walk in, push 'Main Floor,' and everything else goes blank."

He went out the door, refusing to dignify their jeers by any defense, and made for the elevators. By the time he reached the corner of the hall, he had slipped into his topcoat. He pushed the button to call the elevator.

When it arrived, Colborn stepped inside and rode down to the ninety-fifth floor. He switched to a public express elevator, which picked up several other people before becoming an express at the seventy-fifth floor.

"Lived through it again," he muttered to a man next to him as they reached the main floor.

He joined the growing stream of office workers flowing through the lobby of the building, taking for granted the kaleidoscopic play of decorative lights on the translucent ceiling. He noticed them when they suddenly went out.

There was first silence, then a babble of voices until small emergency lights went on. Someone spoke of a fuse blowing. Colborn looked outside, and saw no street lights or illuminated signs. His first thought was power for his set upstairs.

"No, that's special," he told himself, "but I'd better call and see if the elevators are working."

SIX

FOR A JAIL CELL, THE CHAMBER WAS QUITE commodious. The walls were of bare stone, like most of the buildings on Greenhaven which Maria Ringstad had visited during her short period of sightseeing. She thought that it must have entailed a great deal of extra labor to provide such large rooms in a stone building, especially when the materials had to be quarried by relatively primitive means.

On Greenhaven, everything had evidently been done the hard way. She had heard about that facet of the Greenie character before leaving the ship, and she now wished that she had listened more carefully. It was difficult to picture in her mind just how far away that spaceship was by this time.

That had been the worst, the feeling of having been abandoned.

Meanwhile, having turned up her nose at the sewing chores

they had assigned to her but having nothing else to occupy her, she sat on the edge of the austere wooden shelf that doubled as a bed and a bench. The Greenie guard standing in the doorway looked as if he had expected to find the sewing done.

"Can't you understand, honey?" said Maria lightly. "You can cart that basket of rags away. I have no intention of sticking my fingers with those crude needles you people use."

The Greenie was a short, sturdy young man, uniformed in the drabbest of dun-colored clothing. A shirt with a high, tight collar starched like cardboard held his chin at a dignified elevation. It also seemed to keep his eyes wide open, Maria thought, unless that was his naturally naive expression.

"Did anyone ever tell you those hats would make good spittoons?" she asked.

"It is forbidden to speak vainly of any correction official," said the young man stiffly.

"Correction official!" echoed Maria. "Look, honey, don't kid with me! I bet you're just a janitor here. If I thought you were a real official, who might be cuddled into letting me out of this cage, I'd be a lot more friendly."

She gave him an amiable grin. It was not returned.

The Greenie stood gripping the thick edge of the blank wooden door until his knuckles whitened. He looked like a man who had just discovered a worm in his apple. Half a worm, in fact.

"Now, I may be pushing thirty-five," said Maria, "but I *know* I don't look *that* bad. Actually, alongside your Greenie girls, I stack up pretty well, don't you think? For one thing, I'm shorter than you are. For another, I fill out my clothes and don't look like a skinny old horse."

"You . . . you . . . are not . . . dressed as an honest woman," the guard got out.

Sitting on the edge of the wooden bunk, Maria crossed her knees—and thought he would choke. She tugged slightly at the short skirt that had attracted so many lowering stares when she had strolled down the main street of First Haven. She was used to being among men, but this poor soul was outside her experience.

Maria Ringstad was aware of both her visual shortcomings and attractions. After a month here, her hair was beginning to grow in darker and less auburn. She was a trifle solid for her five-feet-four, but that came of having a durable frame. Her face was squarish, with a determined nose, and her hazel eyes looked green in some lights. On the other hand, she had a nice smile, and she had spent much time in places where few women went. She was used to being

41

popular with the opposite sex, even in face of competition from members of her own. In the Greenie women, with their voluminous, drab dresses and hangdog expressions devoid of the least make-up, she saw little competition.

"Really," she said, "no one else would think of me as a criminal. I just tried to buy a picture in that little shop. Then the heavens fell in on me."

"The heavens do not fall on Greenhaven," said the guard firmly.

"Well, anyway, some very sour characters trumped up all sorts of charges against me, and here I am. But I didn't *do* anything!"

"The attempt is equal to the deed!"

Maria shook her head and sighed. She stood up and took a few steps toward him.

"You must keep your place," ordered the young man, with an undercurrent of panic in his tone. "I have not come to debate justice with you. You have sinned and you have been sentenced."

I bet he'd faint if I threw my arms around him, thought Maria.

"But what was the sin, honey?" she demanded. "You'd think I'd written a bad article about Greenhaven for my syndicate. Honestly, I didn't even have time to see the place."

The young man released the edge of the door, but still looked worried.

"Greenhaven was founded by colonists who sought liberty and were willing to create a haven for it by the sweat of their brows," he informed her. "Conditions were inhospitable. There were plagues to test their faith and ungainly beasts to test their courage. What has been built here has been built by a great communal struggle, and it is not to be hazarded by the sinful attitudes of old Terra, and—you should have paid the listed price."

"But he wouldn't sell me one at that price when I offered it!"

"Then he did not have one. You attempted to bribe him."

"Well, it was just a friendly offer," said Maria, straightening her skirt. "It didn't amount to anything."

"On the contrary, it amounted to bribery, immorality, and economic subversion. Procedures such as purchase and merchandising must be strictly regulated for the good of the community. We cannot permit chaos to intrude upon the peace of Greenhaven."

"You know, honey," she remarked, studying him with her head cocked to one side, "you talk like a book. A very old book."

The guard rolled his eyes toward the hall. He relaxed for the first time, in order to lean back and listen to something in the corridor.

"I must caution you to cease addressing me as 'honey,' " he said in a lower voice. "I hear the steps of my superior."

Maria laughed, a silvery ripple that made the young man grit his teeth.

"Maybe he's jealous," she suggested. "Or bored. What do you fellows have to do, anyway, except go around handing out cell work and picking it up?"

"There is no place on Greenhaven for idle hands," said the young man, eyeing the untouched sewing with disapproval.

"Isn't there ever any excitement? How often does someone try to escape?"

"It is forbidden to escape," said the guard soberly. He looked as if he wished that he himself could escape.

Heavy steps halted outside the door of the cell to signal the arrival of the chief warden. The latter turned a severely inquiring stare upon the young man, who hastily stepped aside to admit his chief.

"Have you been conversing with the prisoner?" asked the older man.

He was clad in a similar uniform with, perhaps, a slightly higher collar. His dark-browed features reflected greater age and asceticism. Otherwise, Maria thought ruefully, there was little to choose between them. He seemed to have a chilling effect upon the guard.

"Only in the line of duty, sir," the young man responded.

The warden spotted the basket of undone work. He frowned.

"This should have been attended to long ago," he said. "What excuse can there be?"

Maria planted both hands on her hips.

"Plenty!" she announced. "In the first place, you have no right to hold a Terran citizen in a hole like this. In the second, that ridiculous five year sentence is going to be appealed and cancelled as soon as the Terran consul gets things moving."

"That is at least doubtful," retorted the warden, favoring her with a wintry smile which raised the corners of his mouth an eighth of an inch. "Meanwhile, there are methods we can use to enforce obedience. Would you rather I summon some of the women of the staff?"

"I'd rather you'd explain to me what was so awful about trying to buy a picture of the city in that little shop? If they weren't for tourists to buy, why did they have them?"

"Such nonsensical objects are provided for tourists and

43

others who must from time to time be admitted to Green-haven. That does not excuse flouting our laws and seeking to cause dissatisfaction through the example of bribery. The city of First Haven has been wrung from the wilderness, but the struggle to complete our building of the colony must not be hindered or subverted. It is necessary—"

"Aw, hell! You talk like a book too!" exclaimed Maria.

The two men stared at her, silent, wide-eyed, utterly shocked at this open evidence of dementia.

"The price list is sacred to you," she snapped, "but it's all right to put that junk on sale to clip the tourists, isn't it? Why doesn't that strike you as being immoral? They're no good, but their money is, is that it?"

She turned and stalked back to the shelf-bed, where she sat down and deliberately crossed her legs.

"You will not be required further," the warden told the young man. "See that you spread not the plague by repeating any of this Jezebel's loose talk!"

The guard left hurriedly. Maria discovered the warden gaping at her knees, and defiantly tossed her head.

"You never see a leg before?" she demanded. "Or are all the Greenie girls bowlegged? Is that why they wear those horrible Mother Hubbards?"

She gave her skirt a malicious twitch, revealing a few more inches of firm thigh. The warden began to turn red. He muttered something that actually sounded closer to a prayer than a curse, and turned his eyes away.

"I hope those in authority will yield to the importunities of your depraved fellow who calls himself the Terran consul, and sullies the clean air of Greenhaven by his very— I hope they do deport you!"

"Oh, honey! Could you arrange it?" cried Maria, leaping up and advancing on him.

She grabbed him just above the elbows, and he broke her hold by sweeping both hands upward and outward. This offered Maria the opportunity to take a double grip upon his belt. When he lowered his hands to free himself, she threw both arms about his neck.

"I knew someone could fix things up!" she exclaimed. "You're going to let me out of here until they decide what ship to put me on, aren't you?"

The warden's expression was horror-stricken. With a heavy effort, he got both hands against her and shoved. Maria staggered back all the way to the bunk. The warden, apparently not quite sure what he had done, looked down at his hands. He turned them palm up, then, as his gaze met Maria's, made as if to thrust them behind his back.

"Relax, honey," she said. "You were a little high. I don't imagine you have any laws here against shoving a lady on her can—as long as you're careful where you shove."

"May the Founders protect me from a forward woman!" breathed the warden. "Will you be still and listen to me, Jezebel? Or would you continue ignorant of the news I brought?"

"What news?"

"I am instructed to inform you that you have an official visitor. Do you wish to see him?"

Maria shoved herself away from the edge of the bunk and assumed a dignified stance. She tugged her clothing into order.

"I should be most honored to receive this visitor," she said in her best imitation of Greenie formality. "I deeply appreciate your announcing his presence—at last!"

The warden glared at her. Finding no words worthy of the state of his blood pressure, he stepped back and slammed the heavy door shut. It muffled somewhat his departing footsteps.

"I'm out!" yipped Maria.

She did a little jig, ran to the door to press an ear against it, and turned to survey the cell with the fingers of one hand beating a light tattoo against her lips.

She crossed to the bunk. From beneath it, she dragged the small overnight bag she had succeeded in obtaining from the ship before it had left for the next planet. She began to go about the room, collecting the few odds and ends she possessed and packing them.

She was fingering the bristles of her toothbrush for dampness when she heard returning footsteps.

The hell with brushing my hair, she thought. *I'll go as is.*

She threw the toothbrush into the bag, tossed her hairbrush on top, and snapped the catch. She considered herself ready.

The door opened and the warden ushered another man into the cell. Maria felt a sudden chill.

The newcomer was a Greenie.

She looked over his shoulder, hoping for a glimpse of the Terran consul, but there were just the two Greenies facing her. The stranger was nearer in age to the young guard than to the warden. On the other hand, the severity of his expression was a challenge to the older man. The uniform was about the same.

"My name is John Willard," he announced flatly.

He reached into an inner pocket to produce a fold of papers. At the edge of one, Maria caught sight of what she

45

guessed to be an official seal. Willard opened the papers and turned to the warden.

"You identify the prisoner before us as one Maria Ringstad, native of Terra?"

"I do!" said the warden, righteously.

"You will please sign this statement to that effect!"

There was silence in the cell as the warden held the document against the door to scribble his signature. Maria watched in growing chagrin. Willard folded the statement of identification, returned it to his pocket, and faced her.

"Maria Ringstad," he said, "I am to inform you that your appeal has been denied. You will accompany me to Corrective Farm Number Five, where I will deliver you to the authorities who will supervise the serving of your sentence."

Maria dropped her bag.

"*What?* You're lying! Let me see those phony papers! This is some sort of—"

Willard let her have the back of his left hand across the face. Maria never saw it until she was falling. She sat down with a thump, her legs stretched out straight before her.

Unbelievingly, she watched Willard sign a copy of his order for the warden. The latter examined it with satisfaction before tucking it away. They turned to look down at her, and Willard announced that he was ready to leave.

He seemed to think that a good way to forestall an argument was to get her moving as quickly as possible. He yanked on one elbow, the warden pulled on the other, and Maria headed for the door at a smart trot, wondering how she had risen.

"My bag!" she protested.

"I have it," said Willard.

"Turn left for the stairs," said the warden.

"I'm not going!" she yelled.

"Yes, you are," said Willard.

"Yes, you are!" echoed the warden.

They reached the head of the stairs, where the warden released his grip. Willard shoved her forward, and the two of them descended with breakneck lack of balance. At the bottom, they paused for the warden to catch up.

Maria seized the chance to kick Willard in the shin. He turned white, but urged her on as the warden led the way through a barred door into an open courtyard. They crossed the courtyard by fits and starts, with Maria expressing her opinion in words she had never before uttered. The meaning of certain of them still eluded her, but Willard seemed to understand the general drift.

The warden spoke to a guard, ordering him to open the

main gate. Willard boosted her through with a knee in the behind. The massive portal swung to with a thud, leaving them out in the street.

"I'll be damned if I go to any prison farm!" Maria shouted in his ear. "I demand to see the Terran consul! This is an outrage!"

Willard glared at a passing Greenie who seemed disposed to look on. He tightened his grip on Maria's arm, the better to tow her twenty feet down the street away from the gate. There, he backed her roughly against the blank granite wall.

"If you don't shut your face," he growled between set teeth, "I'll *really* belt you one!"

Maria gasped in a breath and looked at him. It was easy, since he had thrust his face to within a few inches of hers. Little droplets of perspiration stood out on his forehead.

He looked scared.

SEVEN

WESTERVELT WAS STILL SITTING WITH JOE RO-senkrantz in the communications room when Colborn's call came through. He looked over Joe's shoulder as the operator swiveled to face his telephone viewer.

"How come you remembered the number?" he greeted Colborn. "Did the elevator doors close on you?"

"Very-funny-ha-ha!" retorted Colborn. "Look, Joe—have you got power?"

Westervelt peered closer, thinking that the redhead looked unusually concerned. Rosenkrantz seemed not to have noticed.

"Power?" he said. "Have I got power! I can pull in stations you never heard of, just on willpower! *You*—you poor slob—you don't even remember if you're on your way home or coming to work! What is it now?"

"I'll tell you what it is," shouted Colborn. "It's a power failure! They don't even have any lights out in the street. I nearly got trampled to death getting back in the lobby to phone you."

Westervelt and Rosenkrantz looked at each other.

"Come to think of it, Charlie," said the operator, "the lights did blink a minute ago. I wonder if that was our own power taking over for the whole floor?"

The saw Colborn turn his head, and heard him expostulating with someone who plainly was impatient to get into the phone cubicle.

"I'll go check the meters," said Rosenkrantz. "Watch the space set for me, Willie!"

"Whuh-wh-wha?" stuttered Westervelt, groping after him. "Charlie! He went away! What do I do if a call comes in?"

Colborn finished dealing with his own problem downstairs, and returned his attention to Westervelt. He requested a repeat.

"I said that Joe went around the corner to check the power," babbled the youth. "What do I do if a space call comes in? He said to watch the set."

"Oh," said Colborn. "You see the little red, star-shaped light at the left of the board under the screen?"

"Yeah, yeah! It's out, Charlie!"

"Well, it should be. It's an automatic call indicator set for our code. If it goes on, it shows you're getting a call even if you have the screen too dark or the audio too low to notice. So you look for a green one like it on the other side. . . ."

"Yeah. I see it."

"You push the button beside it, and our code goes out automatically to acknowledge. Then you push the next button underneath, which puts out a repeating signal to stand by. Got that so far?"

"I got it," said Westervelt. "Then what?"

"Then you go scream for Joe at the top of your lungs. That covers everything. You are now a deep-space operator. Just don't touch any of those buttons until you get a license!"

"But, Charlie—!"

He was saved by the return of Rosenkrantz, for whom he thankfully vacated space before the phone. Colborn was again engaged in making faces at some other desperate commuter.

"You were right, Charlie," said Rosenkrantz. "We're strictly on our own private power. The whole floor, as near as I can tell. I thought they were being fussy when they put it in, but maybe it will pay off at that. How does it look down there?"

"It's a mess," said Colborn. "You wouldn't believe there were so many people working in our building."

"No, no!" said Rosenkrantz. "I mean, what's the situation? Is it just this building that's cut off, or the whole city, or what?"

"You can't believe anything they're saying," Colborn told

48

them, "but they had somebody yapping on the public address system. It seems there's a whole section of the city, about fifty blocks square, cut off. They're talking about a main cable overloading."

"I can imagine what they're saying," said Rosenkrantz. "The poor guys stuck with finding and replacing it, I mean."

Colborn gave a hollow laugh.

"You think they're the only ones stuck? There ain't a single subway belt moving to the surburban heliports. All the local surface monorails are stopped. You should see the way they're packing the ground taxis, and the cops won't let any more helicabs come down."

"They're supposed only to pick up from the roofs," said Rosenkrantz.

"That isn't where the people are. The people are all down here with me, and half of them are trying to get in the booth to tell their wives they won't be home. Well, there's a lot of us won't get home tonight, if the boys don't find that break pretty soon."

Westervelt and Rosenkrantz exchanged glances. The youth shrugged; he had been planning on staying late anyhow.

"Tell him to come back up, Joe," he suggested. "We have food in the locker for visitors, and he can clear a table in here to snooze on."

Colborn had heard him, and was shaking his head.

"I'd like nothing better, Willie," he said, "but I might as well start walking. It's better on the level than on the stairs."

"What do you mean—stairs?"

"I don't know about the other buildings around here, but they regretfully announced that there will be no elevators running above the seventy-fifty floor in this one. In fact, they only have partial service that high, on the building's emergency power generator."

Rosenkrantz looked worried. Broodingly, he fumbled out a box of cigarettes.

"What do you think, Charlie?" he asked. "I mean . . . Lydman."

"That's why I called," said Colborn. "I think you better check the stairs and tell Smith. If he starts our boy down them, the ninety-nine floors will give him something to keep his mind busy."

The pressure from outside finally intimidated him into switching off. The last they saw of him on the fading phone screen, he was striving desperately to ease himself out of the booth in the face of a bellowing rush of harried commuters

49

for the phone. Joe sighed, trying to light his smoke from the wrong end of the box.

"I'm going to check our elevator, Joe," Westervelt said.

He left the communications room and trotted up the corridor and around the corner. Through the main doors, he caught sight of Pauline peering out of her compartment. A thought struck him.

He hurried over to her and thrust his head close to the opening in her glass partition.

"Were you still on that line, Cutie?" he demanded.

"What line?" demanded Pauline indignantly. "Oh, Willie, does this mean we have to walk down twenty-five floors tonight?"

"You little—Listen! Don't let out a peep about this until we know more!"

"Why not, Willie?"

"Do you want to get everybody upset? How can they dream up brilliant ideas while they're worrying about ordering sandwiches sent up? Promise!"

Pauline reluctantly gave her word not to say anything without consulting him. Westervelt returned to the hall, where he pressed the button for the elevator.

He waited about three times as long as it usually took to get a car, then tried again with the same lack of results. Looking up, he discovered that even the red light over the entrance to the stairs was out. That, apparently, had not been part of ninety-ninth floor system now powered by their own generator.

Westervelt took the few steps to the doorway concealing the stairs. There was a beautifully reproduced notice on the door, informing all persons that this was an emergency exit and that the door would open automatically in case of fire or other emergency. It further offered detailed directions on how to leave, which in simple language meant "go downstairs."

"The door is shut," muttered Westervelt, "so that proves there isn't any emergency."

He tried the handle. It did not budge, except for a slight clicking.

Feeling slightly uneasy, he leaned over to squint at the crack of the door. He spotted the latch, a sturdy bar, and saw that he was moving it. There was, however, another bar which did not move, and the door refused to slide open.

"Of course," he breathed. "It's made to open automatically. How would they do that? By electricity. What haven't we

50

got plenty of? The damn' thing's locked! Somebody designed a beautiful set-up!"

He looked about the empty corridor, jittering indecisively. "I could call downstairs before I tell Smitty," he reminded himself.

For the sake of having a handy shoulder to cry on, he went all the way back to the communications room to use a phone. He made a gesture of throwing up his hands as Joe looked around, then got Pauline on the phone.

"See if you can get me the building manager's office," he requested. "Don't be surprised if it's busy for a couple of minutes."

It was nearer fifteen minutes before his call went through. During that time, he learned that Rosenkrantz took a serious view of the inconvenience.

"I guess you heard some of the talk about Bob Lydman," said the operator. "Well, some is imagination, but a lot of it's true. He spent a long time in hellhole out among the stars; and if there's anything that might shove him off course, it's the idea that he can't get *out*. No matter where he is, he has to know he can leave when he feels like it!"

"But if he doesn't know about it?" asked Westervelt.

"How long can you keep it quiet? I bet you can see a blackout from the window. Watch the set—I'll take a look."

"Aw, now, wait a minute, Joe!"

Westervelt's consternation was diverted by the call that came through at that moment. A perspiring face with ruffled gray hair—which Westervelt could remember having seen occasionally about the lobby downstairs, looking extremely sleek and well-groomed—appeared on the phone screen.

"If you're above the seventy-fifth, walk down that far. If you're lower, walk down as far as you can," said the man hoarsely. "If you can stay put, that's the best thing."

"Tell me, what—?"

"Power failure, not responsibility of the building management," said the sweating gentleman. "Please co-operate!"

"But what—?"

"We're doing all we can and this phone is busy, young man! Will you please—"

"The stairs are locked!" shouted Westervelt.

For a moment, he doubted that he had penetrated the official's panic. Then he saw new outrage in the man's eyes.

"What did you say?"

Westervelt explained about the door to the stairs. The gentleman downstairs clapped both hands to his moist cheeks. He had begun to look numb.

After a long pause, he pulled himself together enough to

51

promise that he would look into the matter. As he switched off, Westervelt heard him muttering that it was just too much.

"You hear that, Joe?" he asked.

"Yeah, an' I didn't like it," replied the operator. "What does that leave us . . . no elevators, no stairs . . . how about the helicopter roof?"

"You have to walk up a flight of stairs to get there," said Westervelt, thinking of the department's three helicopters garaged on their private tower roof. "It's the same door. I suppose the door at the top is frozen too."

"Well, anyway, that could be worse," said Joe. "That makes two doors to knock open, an' I bet your boys have some little gadget around that will do that."

Westervelt felt better. There was always a way out, he told himself. Just the same, he thought he had better let Smith know about the situation.

He told Joe where he was going and headed back up the hall. When he reached the corner, he tried the door again for luck. The luck was the same.

He wondered whether to go look in the lab for some burning tool. On second thought, he decided that if any damage had to be done to the building, it was not his responsibility. He turned to enter the main office, flashing Pauline a wink that he hoped would look reassuring.

Simonetta was busy with a case folder but Beryl was seizing an opportunity to repair her nail polish of irridescent gold. She eyed him curiously as he bent over to whisper into the brunette's ear.

"Are they still talking in there, Si?" he asked.

She drew away with a mock frown, demanding, "What's so confidential? Are you spying for Yoleen?"

Westervelt scowled over her head out the window. It was twilight outside, and he noted that there were only a few dim lights in nearby tall buildings.

"I just wanted to see Mr. Smith," he forced himself to say.

"Don't tell me that you want to go home, now that you got all the rest of us to say we'd stay?"

She softened when she saw that he had no wisecrack in readiness.

"You know I didn't mean that, Willie," she said. "Is something the matter?"

Of all the people in the department, Simonetta was the one he found it easiest to confide in. He had to struggle with himself, especially since he saw no reason why she should not know.

"I . . . uh . . . just wanted to see him a minute," he said lamely. "I'll come back later."

52

He got out of the office, feeling his neck burn under the combined stares of the two girls.

In the corridor, he halted to survey the sealed-off means of egress. Both the elevator and the stairway door looked normal enough except for the red exit light being dark. Westervelt wondered if it would be smart to go around and adjust all the window filters so that no one would expect to see many city lights should they happen to glance outside.

He went over to the door for one last examination, wishing that it were a hinged type instead of sliding. While he was bending to peep at the lock, he heard a sound behind him and leaped up guiltily.

Smith stood six feet away, outside the hall door of his office. He had planted one fist on his hip and was running the other hand through his rumpled hair as he gaped at Westervelt.

"There's no keyhole there, Willie," he said at last.

Westervelt had the feeling that he ought to offer the perfectly simple explanation with which he had been living for what seemed like hours. The words refused to come.

"Does this have anything to do with the message Si just brought me?" demanded Smith.

"What message?" asked Westervelt, clearing his throat.

"The police called and claimed someone reported seeing, from the air, three helicopters being stolen from our roof."

"Did she say that?" asked Westervelt.

"She had the sense to write it down and show me while they were talking about submarines. Something about the way she winked made me think I'd better come out, so I told the boys I was going down the hall a minute."

Westervelt heaved a sigh. He would not have to be alert to duck an aroused Lydman charging down the corridor.

"Then, Mr. Smith," he suggested, "let's walk down that way in case someone comes out and sees us, and I'll tell you all about it."

"They shouldn't be out for a while," Smith commented, examining the youth doubtfully. "I started a little argument before I came out."

Nevertheless, he followed Westervelt around the far corner, to the wing leading to the laboratory and rest rooms. They had gone perhaps ten feet past the corner when Westervelt finished the report on the elevators and came to the frozen locks on the stairway door.

Smith stopped in his tracks, as if to run back and check for himself; but restrained himself.

"You're absolutely sure, Willie?" he asked.

"You can check with Joe Rosenkrantz, Mr. Smith. Or you can call the office of the building manager downstairs."

Smith rubbed his high-bridged nose as he pondered. His lips moved, and Westervelt thought he read the name "Lydman." Then Smith checked off on his fingers, muttering, the stairs, elevators, and helicopters.

"No wonder they were stolen," he said. "Someone saw a chance to make some easy money with all the helitaxis taken. The police will find them tomorrow."

"Meanwhile, I guess it's some trouble to us," said Westervelt.

"Yes, it might be some trouble," admitted Smith, and this time said it aloud: "Lydman! We won't mention it to him yet, right, Willie?"

EIGHT

THE ROOM WOULD HAVE BEEN NEARLY A CUBE except for the fact that hardly any parallel lines appeared in its design. The corners were rounded and the ceiling slightly arched. The floor, though much of it was obscured by a plentiful supply of cushions, was obviously several inches higher in the center than where it curved up to meet the walls. All surfaces were the color of old ivory but seemed to be of a more porous material. The cushions could have been cut from slabs of some foamy, resilient substance that had been manufactured in several rather dull colors.

On two of the larger cushions placed end to end, lay a blond man, long and lean. He wore a dark gray coverall that was loose as if he had lost weight. His features had a poor color, a golden tan with something unhealthy underlying it. He was, however, clean and recently shaven, and his hair was cut short, if somewhat raggedly. He stirred, then blinked into the soft light of an elliptical fixture recessed into the ceiling.

With a smothered groan, he came completely awake. Very carefully, as if from long habit of avoiding painful movement, he rolled to his left side and braced one hand against the floor. The effort of sitting up made him bare his clenched teeth.

The grimace was fleeting. He seemed to have some purpose that drove him on to roll completely off the makeshift bed until he knelt with both knees and his left hand on the smooth floor. As he paused to rest, he held his right hand close to his body.

After a moment, he brought his right foot up opposite his left knee. Another rest period, on hand, knee, and foot, was required before he shoved himself away from the floor and slowly stood upright. The ceiling suddenly looked too low.

He was tall, perhaps two inches over six feet. His features were regular without being especially handsome. A man sizing him up might have expected him to weigh about a hundred and ninety pounds, but slight hollows in his cheeks suggested that this would not be true at the moment. His eyes were blue, but the lids drooped and he seemed to focus only vaguely upon his surroundings.

At length, the man turned and walked deliberately to the side of the room where a doorless opening offered egress into what looked like a corridor. The opening was in the shape of an ellipse about five feet high and three wide, beginning a few inches above the floor. He bent to thrust his head into the hall, peering in both directions but taking no heed of faint, scurrying sounds out there. Satisfied, he walked back to his bed, turned over a cushion with his toe, and kicked a small utility bag of gray plastic out into the open.

The man stared at the bag for some minutes before reaching an evidently unwelcome decision. Laboriously, then, he knelt until he could slide one end under a knee and slide open the zipper with his left hand. He pawed out a few items—battery shaver, towel, deck of cards, toothbrush—which he left scattered on the floor as soon as he located the object of his search. This was a many-jointed mechanism of metal that resembled an armored centipede. It was as long as his hand and nearly as broad. He held it in his palm as if wondering what to do with it.

Some slow process of judgment having blossomed in his mind, he turned over the object to press a small stud. The plates of the "belly" parted. From a recess there, he fumbled out a miniature accessory that fitted easily in the palm of his hand. This was round, about an inch thick, and might have been made of black plastic. The man's lips twitched in a tired smile as he hefted it pensively.

Without moving from his kneeling position, he thumbed a nearly concealed switch on the edge of the disk. Within seconds, the thing began to put forth music, a diminutive reproduction of the sound of a full orchestra. The man gradually raised his hand until he held the little player to his ear. His expression remained uncomprehending. He lowered his hand, shrugging slightly, and turned off the music.

Once more, he forced himself laboriously to his feet. Leaving his other belongings on the floor without a backward glance, he strode to the door with the pace of a man who has just walked five or ten miles. His long legs carried him across the distance in only a few steps, but there was a slowness, a heaviness, in their motion that revealed a deep weariness. He raised one foot just high enough to step through the opening into the corridor.

Outside, he turned left and walked along at the same pace, passing several other doors at irregular intervals. That they may have led to other rooms with other occupants seemed to interest him not at all. He neither glanced aside nor paused until he came face to face with a barrier, a wall blocking his path.

It was the first doorway that sported a door, and the latter was closed. It looked to be made of a plastic substance, darker than the ivory walls among which he had thus far moved, but smoother. There was a grilled opening more or less centered, but no other markings.

Nevertheless, the blond man seemed to know where the portal would be fastened. He ran the tips of his fingers along one curved side, as if judging a distance. Juggling the black disk in his hand until the grip suited him better, he pressed a second switch, which was concealed at the center of the object.

A thin jet of flame, so white that it far outshone the lighting of the corridor, flared against the edge of the door. He moved the flame along the edge for about two feet. Then he snapped it out and waited with his eyes blinking painfully. The corridor lighting had been revealed to be yellow and dim.

Having rested, the man took a deep breah and shoved with his left shoulder against the elliptical door. It slipped off whatever had been holding it at the opposite edge and fell into the hallway beyond the bulkhead. He had neatly cut through two hinges on the other side.

Without looking back, he stepped over the loose door and continued on his way. Eventually, he came to another such barrier, and he dealt with it in the same fashion. The third time he was halted, he found himself at a vertical column which passed down through an oval opening in the ceiling and disappeared through another in the floor of the corridor.

The man hesitated. A vague sadness flitted across his features. Then, as if driven by some deep purpose, he approached the column.

56

It was about six inches in diameter, and the most regular shape he had encountered anywhere. The surface of it was ringed by horizontal grooves nearly an inch deep, and looked as if it would be easy to climb. From the hole below, there rose slightly warmer air, bearing a blend of pungent and musty odors. The man's nostrils wrinkled.

He stepped to the edge of the opening, then sidled around until he had the greatest possible space on his side of the column. The instrument in his hand finally came to his attention as he reached out to touch the grooved surface. He considered it for a long moment. Apparently, he was pleased at the brilliance of the thought that eventually moved him to thrust the thing into a pocket of his pants. He faced the column again, and again hesitated. His right hand lifted an inch, indecisively, following which a snarl of pain twisted his lips.

Sidling around the opening once more until he found himself having completed a circuit, he let the fingers of his left hand explore the grooves. It did not seem to occur to him to look either down or up, although faint, distant sounds were borne to him on the current of odoriferous air.

In the end, he leaned forward until his left shoulder came against the slim column. He wrapped his left arm about it. A little scrambling, and he had gripped it between his legs. Then a slight relaxation of his hold permitted him to slide gradually downward until he slipped past the floor line. There were only a few inches to spare between his shoulders and the edge of the opening, as if the latter had not been designed for such as he.

The next level into which he descended was dark. He continued to slide cautiously downward.

At the second level below his starting point, there was light. The corridor resembled that in which he had begun his journey. He put out one foot to catch the edge of the opening while he rested.

This hallway curved not far from the man in one direction, although the other side ran straight for about twenty feet before being closed off by a door similar to the one he had removed. Around the bend floated faint noises suggesting high-pitched conversation, although they came from too far away to reveal the nature of their origin. The tall man kept one eye cocked warily in that direction.

After a few minutes, certain sounds seemed to draw nearer. The chittering "talk" faded, but he could hear more plainly a hushed scuffling that could have been caused by many feet taking short, hurried steps.

The man released his foothold and slid smoothly below

57

the floor level just as moving shadows appeared at the bend of the corridor. He dropped down the column through four more unlighted levels, reaching an atmosphere that held a blend of machine oil along with its other odors.

Light filtered upward with the air currents. Somewhere below was a very bright level, whence came the rhythmic throb of heavy machinery. This did not resemble the sounds of a spaceship, nor yet a Terran factory, but some considerable work was being carried on. He groped out in the darkness for a foothold, got the other foot over, and wearily pushed himself away from the column.

He was on a level so dim that he touched the edge of the floor opening with his toe to make sure of its location before moving off along the corridor.

In the darkness, he went more slowly than before, but made better time than looked possible. Under the circumstances, he reassured himself by stretching out his left hand every few seconds to touch the smooth wall. He walked normally, though not noisily, and his sense of direction was extraordinarily good.

About a hundred yards along a corridor that seemed not to have a single bend or corner, he slowed his pace doubtfully. A few steps more brought him to another closed door. This one, however, yielded to his shove, swinging back to reveal a stretch of tunnel with a bare minimum of illumination oozing from widely spaced ceiling fixtures. Here, he could sense side doorways his fingers had usually missed along the darker stretch.

He had gone another hundred yards and finally passed two cross corridors, before he was again obliged to stop and rest. He slumped against the side wall, favoring his right arm and gazing dully before him.

A few steps further along was one of the typical elliptical doorways. Through this one, some light was reflected to the wall of the corridor. The man stared at it in the way anyone in the dark will turn his eye to light. After several minutes, he moved toward it as if impelled by idle curiosity.

Reaching the opening, he hesitated. A strange expression flickered over his face. The decision to look or not to look was causing him great uneasiness. Finally, he stepped forward and entered a small chamber.

This was evidently located so as to house another slim column that disappeared upward and downward into unknown levels. Several small, oval windows were set just below the ceiling, at a height which presented no particular difficulty to the man when he stepped over to look through them.

The scene that met his eye was a wide corridor, so wide that it might be termed a concourse or even a public square. Members of the public that were to be observed frequenting it were very, very far from being human.

Two of them scurried past his window, clearly illuminated by lights far up in the domed ceiling. They were furry, about five feet tall, lithe and cat-like in their movements. Compared to a human, they were slim and short-bodied. They possessed three arms and three legs, each set being equally spaced about their bodies. Now and then, as they walked with short, rapid steps, frequent joints were apparent in all limbs, showing clearly that they were not just muscular tentacles. From the openings at the apexes of their heads, which must have been mouths, they were streamlined in a fashion that made it more natural to picture them swimming like Terran cuttlefish then climbing up and down thick poles. The three eyes set about each head were low enough to allow for jaw muscles.

The man watched this pair slide down a column set beside the wall that concealed him. Other individuals were scattered about the wide concourse. Almost without exception, they wore nothing more than a pouch secured by a belt just above what would have been the hips in a human. Clothing was made unnecessary by handsome coats of short, honey-colored fur that enhanced their feline air. Sometimes, when one or another bent or twisted, purple skin would show through the fur.

Across the concourse, the man could see open stalls that suggested shops. Most of them were dark inside, with nettings stretched across the fronts. The general atmosphere was not unlike that of a small Terran business section, or even a spaceport terminal, late in the evening with business slack and only night workers about.

Abruptly, those abroad scuttled for the walls. A perfectly good reason for the exodus appeared a moment later, as a column of low, long vehicles dashed from a high-arched tunnel and shot across the open space. Each was three-wheeled and carried half a dozen individuals wearing what resembled thick plastic armor. Cages of metal guarded their heads and they bore weapons like Terran rocket launchers. The convoy passed out of sight before the man could note more.

He retreated thoughtfully from the window. At the opening to the corridor, he paused indecisively. He shook his head as if trying to put out of his mind what he had just witnessed.

It might have been prudent for anyone in his position to give the corridor a searching look before entering, but this did not seem to occur to him. In seconds, he was striding along in the former direction—if anything, a trifle more briskly.

As he walked, the muffled sounds from the scene he had examined faded in the distance. Once again, he was alone with his own discreet footfalls. Several times, he passed junctions of cross corrridors, and once he had to burn open a door; but never did he meet an inhabitant of the hive-like city. Either the way had been shrewdly chosen or it was seldom used at this period of the day. Even granting both, his luck must have been fantastic.

The corridor had begun to assume an almost hypnotic monotony when it ended bluntly at a column leading only upward. The man perforce was faced with the challenge of climbing it, a prospect which he obviously did not relish.

Sighing, he reversed his earlier procedure in sliding down other poles. With only one good arm, pulling himself up was slow work. It was, perhaps, only the fact that the levels were constructed to suit beings five feet tall that made it possible for him to make it to the next level up. He sat with his legs dangling through the opening, panting, while perspiration oozed out to bead his forehead.

This time, he was nearly half an hour in recovering and working up the determination required to go on. The corridor in which he found himself ran at right angles to the one below. It was wider and higher, as if more traveled, but any such open area as he had peeped at was far to the rear. Nearby, however, was a much larger door than he had yet encountered. He walked over to it.

When a tentative push produced no results, he dipped his left hand into a pocket for the black disk.

He seemed to have a good idea of where to locate the hinges on this door too. When he had burned through, the door was harder to shove aside because it turned out to be of double thickness. The hinges had been concealed from both inside and outside. The tall man now found himself only a few steps from another such portal, in what looked like an anteroom.

Methodically, he proceeded to burn his way through, squinting in the bright light of the flame but otherwise betraying no emotion.

The last door fell away. Fresh air billowed in around him, and he could see stars in a night sky outside.

Without haste, he stepped outside.

The tan, plastery wall reared above him for about ten levels. Off to his left, shadows on the ground showed a jagged shape, so it was probable that another part of the building towered

60

upward after a set-back. The ground around the exit was
perfectly level and bare of any vegetation. The nearest life
was a wall of shrub-like trees about a hundred feet away,
and toward these the man began to walk in the same tired
pace.

He found, as if by instinct, a broad, well-kept path through
the trees. A mild breeze caused the long, hanging leaves to
rustle. Without looking back, the man followed the path up
a gentle slope and over the curve of the hill. At the bottom
of the downgrade, two figures shrank suddenly back into the
shadows. He kept walking.

"That you, Gerson?" came a loud whisper, as the two Terrans stepped forward again. "Come on; we have an aircar
over here! Did anyone follow you?"

The tall man turned to go with them through a fringe of
trees. It seemed like a poor time to try to talk, with the possibility of pursuit behind them. The two bundled him into
the black shape of the aircar in silence, and moved it
cautiously through the trees just above the ground. They
raised into clear air only when they had put half a mile
between them and the towering hive-city.

NINE

IN THE LIBRARY, BETWEEN SMITH'S CORNER OFFICE
and the conference room that adjoined the communications
center, Westervelt sat and watched Lydman pore over a technical report in the blue binding of the Department of Interstellar Relations. Half a dozen other volumes, old and new,
technical and diplomatic, were scattered about the table
between them.

The youth caught himself running a hand through his
hair in Smith's usual manner, and stopped, appalled. He
judged, after due reflection, that it might be worse: he could
have picked up some of Lydman's peculiarities instead.

Probably, he told himself, he ought to show some better
sense and imitate the suavity of Parrish if he had to adopt
the manners of anyone in the department. Unfortunately, he
did not like Parrish very well, even when he was not engaged in being actively jealous of the man.

Some day, Willie, he mused, you'll snap too. When you

do, it would be just your style to take after this mass of beef front of you.

Immediately, he was ashamed of the thought. Lydman had been, in his way, nicer to him than anyone else. Moreover, he was far from being a mass of beef. Westervelt recalled the sight of Lydman on an open beach, where he seemed more at ease than anywhere else. The man kept himself hard-muscled and trim. Despite the gaunt look that sometimes crossed his features, he was probably on the low side of thirty.

So he's still quick as well as strong, thought Westervelt. *If he does go for the door the way Joe predicts, Willie my boy, you be sure to get out of the way!*

In theory, he was supposed to be helping Lydman research some problems Smith had thought up. So far, he had read one short article which had bored the ex-spacer and twice gone to the files for case folders. He was very well aware that the real idea was to have someone with Lydman constantly. For this reason, he was prepared further to assume the courtesy of answering any interrupting phone calls. He was determined that any news not censored by Pauline would be a wrong number, no matter if it were the head of the D.I.R. himself.

Lydman looked up from his reading.

"I'm getting hungry; aren't you, Willie?"

"I guess so. I didn't notice," said Westervelt.

"How about phoning down for something? Get whatever you like."

That was typical of Lydman, Westervelt realized. The man did not care what he ate. Smith would have been specific though unimaginative. Parrish would have sent instructions about the seasoning. The girls would choose something sickening by Westervelt's standards. He shoved back his chair and stood up.

"I'd better see what they're doing up front," he said. "I think Mr. Smith was talking about it being quicker to raid our own food locker. I'll be back in a minute."

Lydman raised his gray-blue eyes and stared through him curiously.

"No hurry," he said mildly.

Westervelt thought that the man was still watching him as he walked through the door, but he did not like to look back. It might have been so.

When he reached the main office, he found both girls replacing folders in the bay of current files opposite Simonetta's desk.

"How about letting me at the buried treasure?" he asked. "The thought of food is infiltrating insidiously."

"Willie," said Simonetta, "you'll go far here. None of the other brains had such a good idea. I'll phone for something if you'll see what people want."

"I think Mr. Smith wants to use stuff we have in the locker," said Westervelt, blocking the way to her desk. "Hold it a second while I check."

He rapped on Smith's door as he opened it. He found the chief with most of the papers on his desk shoved to one side so that a built-in tape viewer could be brought up from its concealed position. Smith was scowling as if obtaining little useful information from whatever he was watching.

"They're getting hungry," Westervelt whispered. "Is it all right to raid our guest locker?"

Smith shut off his machine, and scrubbed one hand across his long face.

"Right, Willie," he agreed. "The sooner the better. Take out whatever you think best and pass it around. Meanwhile, I'd better check on the situation downstairs—come to think of it, when you called, did you get an outside line and punch the numbers yourself?"

"No, but I have an understanding with Pauline," said Westervelt.

He was thinking that Smith had put him in charge of the food, which was perhaps a little better than being sent around to take personal orders as the girls had assumed he would do, but which was still a long way beneath the conference status he had appeared to have an hour earlier.

"Good boy!" Smith approved. "Then she'll know who I want to talk to and that she shouldn't listen in."

Westervelt was far from sanguine about the last condition, but left without trying to cause his chief any unhappiness.

Well, so it goes, he reflected. *One minute a project man, the next an office boy! If I pick out what everybody likes, I'll be a project man again. But if they like it too much, I'll turn out to be the official chef around here whenever someone important stays to lunch.*

The picture of sitting in on a talk with some potent official of the D.I.R. and expounding his brilliant solution to a problem, only to be requested to slap together a short order meal, made him pause outside the door, frowning.

"Now what, Willie?" asked Simonetta.

He roused himself.

"Leave it to me, Si," he answered, working up a grin. "I have everything under control."

"I hope you know what you're doing," Beryl commented.

63

"I won't stand for a plate of mashed potatoes and gravy, or anything that fattening."

"You'll have your choice," Westervelt promised. "I wouldn't want anything to spoil that figure. Just let me at the locker."

He slipped an arm around her waist to move her aside. The flesh of her flank was softly firm under his fingers, and he made himself think better of an impulse to squeeze.

Beryl stepped away, neither quickly enough to be skittish nor slowly enough to imply permissiveness. Westervelt shrugged. He stepped forward to the blank wall at the end of the file cabinets, and slid back a panel to reveal a white-enameled food locker.

It was divided into an upper and lower section, with transparent doors that rolled around into the side walls. The lower half was refrigerated. Westervelt opened the upper to explore more comfortably.

Most of the foiled packages contained sandwiches, many of them self-heating. Somewhat bulkier containers held more substantial delicacies: Welsh rabbit, turkey and baked potato, filett mignon, rattlesnake croquettes, and salmon salad. There were sealed cups of coffee, tea, or bouillon that heated themselves upon being opened, and ice cream and fruits in the freezer section.

"Si, let me have a couple of 'out' baskets," said Westervelt, holding out his hand.

"Empty?"

"All right—your 'in' and Beryl's 'out' trays. Do you expect me to go around with everybody's supper stuffed in my pockets?"

"Frankly, yes," said Beryl. "But not with mine. Let me see what they have in there!"

She examined the array while Westervelt experimented with balancing two empty desk trays across his forearm. By the time he was ready, the girls had blocked him off, and he had to wait until the possibilities had been debated thoroughly. In the end, Simonnetta selected veal scallopini; and Beryl took a crabmeat sandwich for herself and a filet mignon for Parrish. Westervelt grinned when he saw that she also chose four sealed martinis.

His own decisions were simple. Putting aside a budding curosity about rattlesnake meat, he took a package of fried ham and eggs—to see if it could be possible—and a self-heating package of mince pie. For Smith, Lydman, and Rosenkrantz, he piled a tray with half a dozen roast beef or turkey sandwiches, a selection of pie and ice cream, and all the coffee containers he could fit in.

"Si, pick out something nice for Pauline," he requested,

noting that Beryl was already on the way across the office to Parrish's door.

Simonetta exclaimed at her forgetfulness, pushed aside the container that she had been warming on her desk according to instructions, and told him to go ahead.

"I'll take her a salad and some bouillon," she said. "The kid thinks she has to watch her weight already."

As an afterthought, Westervelt topped his load with a martini for Smith, on the theory that the chief was going to need it.

He went in there first, let Smith see that nothing but coffee was on the way to Lydman, and made his exit directly into the hall. He made the communications room his next stop, and took what was left into the library to share with Lydman.

The latter took a roast beef sandwich, pulled the heating tab, and tore it open after the required thirty seconds with one twist of his powerful fingers. Westervelt had a little more trouble with his package of ham and eggs, but the coffee cups were simpler.

They sat there in silence, except for an occasional word, and a brief scramble when Westervelt spilled coffee on a list of cases Lydman had thought of for further checking. The ex-spacer chewed methodically on three sandwiches, and poured down two containers of coffee, scanning a copy of the *Galatlas* all the while.

Westervelt found the fried ham and eggs to be a disappointment.

I should have tried a steak, he reflected. *Eggs can't be done. Not and taste right.*

There was one sandwich left, cold turkey, and Lydman had just begun on his third, so the youth helped himself. The hot mince pie had real flavor, and he was feeling quite comfortable by the time Lydman finished his ice cream.

"Shall I get some more coffee?" Westervelt offered.

"Not for me," said the other. "If you go back, though, you could pick up those folders."

Westervelt took the excuse to leave for a few minutes. He stopped in to see if Joe wanted anything, promised to look for bourbon, and returned to the main office. He found Simonetta sipping a solitary cup of coffee.

"Did they leave you all alone?" he demanded.

"Oh, no," she said. "The boss came out and had coffee with Pauline and me, but then she had a call for him and he thought he'd rather take it in his office."

Westervelt stepped over to Smith's door and listened. In theory, it should have been soundproof, so he opened it a

65

crack. Hearing Smith's voice, he pushed his luck and put his head inside. The chief was busy enough on the phone not to be aware of the intrusion.

"Yes, I appreciate your difficulty," Smith said, obviously having said it many times before. "Still, if there is no way to send us an elevator, I would much rather not have a party climbing the twenty-five flights to break open the door. If it has to be broken, we can do it."

Westervelt recognized the answering voice, hoarser though it now was, as that of the silver-haired manager downstairs. He wondered why the sight of each other did not make both the manager and Smith want to comb their hair.

"Naturally, we will make good any damage," Smith said. "Besides, you must have a good many other people on the lower floors of the tower to look after."

"Most of them are displaying the good sense to stay in their offices until the emergency is dealt with."

Westervelt crept inside and moved around until he could see the face pouting on the screen of Smith's phone. The man now had heavy shadows under his eyes, although he had mopped off the perspiration that had bathed him when Westervelt had spoken with him.

"Well, perhaps we have slightly different problems," Smith told the manager.

"Problems!" exclaimed the latter. His effort to contain his emotions was clearly visible. "Well . . . of course . . . if it is really serious, perhaps we can get the police to send up an emergency rescue squad—"

"No!" Smith interrupted violently. "No rescue squad! We do not in any way need to be rescued. Not at all!"

The manager eyed him with dark suspicion.

"Is someone ill?" he demanded. "We cannot be responsible for any lawsuits due to your refusal to let us call competent authorities."

"Aren't you a competent authority?" demanded Smith. "Just get the elevator working, will you? We'll wait until then."

"There is no way of knowing when power will be restored," said the manager. "You must have a TV set around the office somewhere, so you can hear the news bulletins on the situation as soon as I can." He paused to pop a lozenge into his mouth, sighed, and added, "Sooner, I dare say."

Smith had leaned back in his chair, a stricken look on his face. He saw Westervelt, and began to wave frantically toward the hall.

"I never thought of that," exclaimed the youth.

He burst into the hall from Smith's private entrance,

66

realized he would have to pass the library to reach Joe Rosen-krantz with an order for censorship, and circled back to the main entrance.

He went in, saw Simonetta still at her desk, and opened the door to Pauline's cubicle. When he got inside with the little blonde, her swivel chair, and her switchboard, there was just about room enough to breathe.

"Pauline!" he panted. "Punch the com room number and lend me your headset!"

"This is cosy!" she giggled, but did as he asked.

Joe answered promptly.

"Joe, this is Willie. It just so happens that Charlie Colborn was changing transistors in all the personal sets you have down there, so you can't pick up a newscast right now—right?"

There was a pregnant pause before one answered.

"Right. That's the way it goes. Can you talk? I don't see any image."

"I'm with Pauline. It's okay. I mean, it was just a thought, in case. . . ."

"Sure," said Rosenkrantz. "Should have thought of it myself. Everything else all right?"

Westervelt told him that it was, agreed that he hoped it would continue. Then he surrendered the headset to Pauline, who tickled his ribs as he squirmed around to leave the cubicle.

"Don't you dare!" she giggled when he turned on her. "I'll talk!"

"Please, no, Pauline," he sighed. "Anything but that!"

He walked loosely past Simonetta, who stared at him un-believingly, and started to enter Smith's office again. Behind him, he heard the sounds of a door being closed and high heels clicking subduedly on the springy flooring. Beryl's voice said something as he began to look around. He stopped.

"What did she say?" he asked Simonetta.

Beryl had already disappeared toward the hall.

"She said Mr. Parrish invited her downstairs for a cocktail. He thinks they should have about twenty minutes to relax before going back to work."

"You're kidding!" gasped Westervelt.

"No, I'm not! Willie, you've been acting awfully strange. Where have you been ducking to every time—"

Westervelt was already running for the hall.

He skidded and nearly fell going through the entrance. Beryl was standing near the elevator.

"Did you ring yet?" asked Westervelt.

"No, I'm waiting for Mr. Parrish," said Beryl, in a tone that emphasized unwieldiness of an assembly of three persons.

"Your lipstick is smeared," said Westervelt.

Beryl gave him an even less believing stare than had Simonetta but, glancing hastily at her watch, began to fumble out her compact.

"In here, where the light is better," said Westervelt.

He grabbed her by an elbow and dragged her into the office before it occurred to her to resist.

"Please, Willie! You're *handling* me!" she protested coldly.

Westervelt was already out the door again, bent upon taking the other entrance to Smith's office, when he saw the hall door of Parrish's office open. He reversed direction in time to meet Parrish as the latter stepped into the corridor.

"Beryl said to tell you she'll be right back," he said, waving a thumb vaguely in the direction of the rest rooms.

"Oh. Thanks, Willie," answered Parrish. "I'll wait inside."

Westervelt reached Smith's office before Parrish had completely closed his own door. From the corner of his eye, he saw the blue of Beryl's dress.

"Mr. Smith!" he called as he thrust his head inside. "I think I need help!"

TEN

THE FIRST SENSATION THAT PENETRATED, AGONIzingly, to Taranto's consciousness was that of heat. Heat, and then the damp itch of soaking sweat.

The next feeling, as he groggily sought to take up the slack in his hanging jaw, was thirst. It was a raging demand that brought him entirely awake. Before he could control himself, he had emitted a groan.

Immediately, he was dropped from whatever had been supporting him in a swaying, dipping fashion. He landed with a thud on the hard ground.

A chatter of Syssokan broke out above him. It was answered by other Syssokan voices farther away. Taranto kept his eyes closed and lay limply where he had sprawled, while he tried to figure out what had gone wrong.

Shortly before dawn, he and Meyers had each swallowed his capsule as directed. He remembered a period of vague

68

drowsiness after that, then nothing more until he had been awakened just now. From his still dizzy mind, he sought to drag the outline of events expected.

They had hoped to be taken out to the desert, possibly to a Syssokan burial ground according to the local custom, and left to be dried by the dessicating blaze of the sun. It had been planned that a spaceship would land in the late afternoon to pick them up: Undoubtedly, it would take the Syssokans several hours to report the "deaths" and to secure official permission for disposal of the bodies, even though they were less given to red tape than Terrans. Still, they should have abandoned the "bodies" long before Taranto had expected to awake.

He risked opening one eye a slit. Syssokan legs crowding around blocked his view, but he could tell that it was dusk. The heat he felt must be that of sand and rocks that had baked all day.

It must have taken the Syssokans a long time to get this far. He wondered whether they had brought him an unusual distance into the desert, perhaps to avoid contaminating their own burial grounds, or whether they had simply indulged in some long-winded debate as to the proper course to pursue in regard to deceased aliens.

My God! he thought. *What if they'd decided to dissect us? I never thought of that! I wonder if the joker that sent those pills did?*

Whatever had gone wrong, he was well behind schedule. He could imagine the chagrin of the D.I.R. man watching the proceedings through his little flying spy-eye. Taranto hoped that the spacers hired for the pick-up were still standing by—at the worst, they would have water. Cautiously, he tried to move his tongue inside his mouth. It stuck against his teeth. He suspected that the taste would be terrible, if he could taste at all.

The heat! he thought. *I've been soaking up heat all day and not sweating. Now it's jetting out of every pore.*

Whatever the drug had done or failed to do, it must have nearly suspended most of the normal functions of the body. No wonder he was perspiring so heavily as he began to recover! Even so, he felt as if he had a fever. He began to hope that he had not been carried for very long. Unless he had been lying in the cell—or, better, in some examination room at ground level—for most of the elapsed time while disputes held up disposal of his body, some instinct told him, he was very likely to die.

Someone rubbed a hand roughly over his face, slipping through the film of sweat. At this demonstration, renewed exclamations broke out above him. One of the Syssokans shouted some gabble, as if to another some way off.

A moment later, Taranto heard a hoarse yelp that could have come only from a Terran throat. Then words began to form, and he realized that it must be Meyers.

That blew the pipes! he thought, and opened his eyes.

A Syssokan looking down at him hissed in astonishment. Others, who had been watching another group about twenty feet away, turned to stare down at Taranto. He was hauled to his feet by the first pair that thought of it. One, a minor officer by his red uniform, sputtered a question at the Terran, forgetting in his evident excitement that he was speaking Syssokan. Taranto wiped his face with his shirtsleeve. He was beginning to feel a trifle cooler as his perspiration evaporated in the dry air, but his surroundings seemed feverishly unreal.

He could not quite understand what Meyers was shouting now, but even in the hoarse voice could be detected a note of pleading. Taranto thought it must be something about water. The Syssokan before him gathered his wits and repeated his question in Terran.

"What doess thiss mean?" he demanded, glaring angrily at Taranto with his huge, black eyes.

The Terran tried to answer, but could not get the words out. He gestured weakly at a waterskin secured to the harness of one of the soldiers. After a brief moment of hesitation, the officer waved permission. The soldier detached the container and handed it suspiciously to Taranto. Fearing the effect of too much liquid in one jolt, the latter forced himself to take only a few small swallows. He wished he could afford to stick his whole head inside the skin and soak up the water like a blotter.

"You are dead!" declared the officer impatiently.

The tiny greenish-gray scales of his facial skin actually seemed ruffled. Taranto dizzily sought for some likely apology to excuse his being alive. He decided that there might be a slim chance of getting away with a whopper.

"If it is officially declared, then of course I am dead!" he croaked. "What d'ya expect. Look how weak I am!"

The Syssokan swiveled their narrow, pointed skulls about at each other.

"I'm in the last minutes," said Taranto sadly.

"What lasst minutess?" asked the officer.

"It's the way Terrans pass on," asserted the spacer. "Didn't you ever see a Terran die?"

The officer silently avoided admitting so much, running

70

a hand reflectively over his thick waist, but his hesitation provided an opening.

"That's the way it goes," said Taranto. "First a blackout . . . we sleep, that is. Then the last minutes, the sweat of death, and . . . blooey!"

He raised the waterskin and sneaked a long swallow, risking it because he feared he might not be allowed another.

He was right. The officer snatched away the skin and thrust it into the long fingers of its indignant owner.

"If you are sso dead," he demanded, not illogically, "why do you drink up our water?"

"Sorry," apologized Taranto. "Where are we?"

"What difference iss it to you?"

"I . . . uh . . . don't want to make hard feelings or bad luck by dying in one of your burial grounds."

"It will not happen," said the officer grimly. "We have been ssent in another place to guard against that. Look back—you can see the city over that way."

Taranto turned. The outline of the city walls, with lights showing here and there on the watch towers, loomed up about five miles away. A small rise in the rolling ground of the desert hid the base of the walls and the greater part of the rough trail they had evidently followed. It would have been a fine spot for a spaceship to drop briefly to the surface.

"Do you wish to lie down here?" asked the officer politely. "We will wait until it iss over."

Don't be so damn' helpful! thought Taranto.

He looked desperately about, striving to give the impression of seeking a comfortable spot. He felt the situation turning more and more sour by the minute. It would be very difficult to feign death successfully again now that the Syssokan suspicions were so aroused. They might well make sure of him in their own way.

Near him stood half a dozen brown-clad soldiers. Four of them, spears slung on their shoulders by braided straps, had apparently been carrying him while two others acted as relief bearers. Besides the officer, there was a sub-officer, also in brown but wearing a red harness. In the background, a similar group clustered about Meyers.

Taranto saw that he had been tumbled from a sort of flat stretcher of wickerwork. It was of careless craftsmanship, as if meant to be abandoned with the body it served on the last journey. He wondered if it could be assumed to be his property.

"Don't put yourselves out," he said. "I can't hardly take a step even to sit down. It'll be just a coupla minutes now. Good-bye!"

71

The Syssokan officer made no move to depart. Taranto had not really dared to hope that he would. He was trying to think of some further excuse when Meyers saved him the trouble.

"*Help!* Taranto!" shrieked the other spacer, bursting suddenly from the group about him. "I told them we're alive, and they want to kill us!"

He ran staggeringly toward Taranto, kicking up spurts of sand. His shirt front was dark with sweat and dribbled water. He looked wild with fright.

"Ah, they do live!" exclaimed the officer. "Seize them!"

He seemed to realize only after about ten seconds that he had, this time, spoken in Terran. Evidently feeling that not all his men might have learned that particular language, he began to repeat the order in Syssokan. Taranto interfered by swinging his fist at the center of the greenish-gray features. The Syssokan, arms flung wide, sailed backward and landed on the nape of his neck in a patch of gravel. Meyers screamed hoarsely as his own bearers caught up to him and dragged him down.

Taranto sprang forward to snatch up the wicker stretcher from the ground. A long-fingered hand clutched at his shoulder, but let go when he kicked backward without looking around. He raised the stretcher and swung it around in a wide arc at the three Syssokans reaching for him.

Two, having left their heads unprotected, went down; but the stretcher frame crumpled. Taranto tripped the other Syssokan, glancing hopefully at the sky. There was no sign of the fire-trail of a descending spaceship in the deepening twilight. Then he had to duck as the other three bearers were upon him.

"Get up, Meyers!" he yelled.

He met the rush with a hard left that dumped the leading Syssokan on his back. The next hesitated, and was brushed aside by the sixth, who had had the wits to unsling his spear.

Taranto sidestepped the crude but large point that thrust straight at his belly. The shaft of the spear slid along his left ribs, and he punched over the outstretched arms of the soldier at the Syssokan's head. He clamped the spear between his elbow and body, retaining it as his attacker staggered back.

Two or three were now advancing from where a knot of figures seemed to be sitting upon Meyers in the gloom. They did not especially hurry. Taranto had begun to reverse the spear to jab at the Syssokan left facing him when he heard a scrabbling behind him.

He whirled away to his right, ducking instinctively as a

body hurtled past him. When he faced about, he found that most of those whom he had knocked down were again on their feet and advancing. The officer, the lower part of his face smeared with purplish blood, ran at Taranto full tilt. He screamed an order in his own language.

The spacer cracked the butt of the spear smartly against the Syssokan's head, sending him down on his face. One of the others, however, managed to get a grip on the weapon. Instinct told Taranto that any attempt at a tug of war on his part would lead to a fatal entanglement. He dodged away and sprinted toward the group pinning Meyers.

A Syssokan voice yelled mushily behind him as he concentrated upon driving with the greatest possible force into the writhing group before him. He struck with a crunch that tumbled bodies in all directions. Taranto himself felt sand scrape raspingly against the side of his face as he half-rolled, half-skidded along the ground.

His pursuers now caught up to the new location of hostilities. The first thing Taranto saw as he managed to drag one knee under him was the butt end of a spear plunging at his midsection. The Syssokan behind it had his center of gravity well ahead of his churning feet, obviously intent upon doing great bodily harm. The spacer wondered for a split second why the native did not use his point.

Then he twisted hips and torso to his right, drawing back his left shoulder. As the spear passed him, he slapped down hard on the shaft with his left hand. The butt dug into the sand, and the Syssokan hissed in consternation as he vaulted head over heels before he could release the weapon. The one immediately behind was caught in the center of his harness by a flying foot, whereupon he collapsed with a groan across the prone figure of his comrade. Two more, who had dropped their spears, reached out toward Taranto, urged on by the officer on their heels.

Taranto saw Meyers stagger to his feet. Then the two Syssokans were all over him. He skipped away to his left over a pair of limp legs, parried a groping hand, and brought around the long, low left hook that had made him respected in past years.

In the ring, he had floored men with that punch. At the least, he expected a fine, loud *whoosh* from the Syssokan, but the latter disappointed him. He folded in limp silence.

For a second or two, everything stopped. Taranto stared down at the soldier, slumped on the ground like a loose sack of potatoes. Even the Syssokans who were not at the moment engaged in pulling themselves to their feet also gaped.

Light dawned for the spacer. Those among whom he had

73

gone head-hunting kept getting to their feet as fast as he knocked them down.

"Hit 'em in the gut!" he yelled to Meyers. "That's where their brains are!"

He charged at the nearest Syssokan, lips drawn back in an unconscious snarl. The soldier made a reflexive motion to cross his arms before his thick abdomen. Taranto, unopposed, hit him alongside the head with a light right, then whipped the left hook in again as the arms began to lift. The Syssokan went out like a light.

"Come on!" Taranto shouted at Meyers when he saw that the other had not moved. "Two of us could do it. Those heads are too little to hold a brain. Kick 'em, if you can't do anything else!"

"Are you crazy?" retorted Meyers, his voice hoarse as much with fear as with thirst. "They'll kill us! Give up, and they'll only take us back!"

Taranto sensed someone behind him. He started to run, but two or three recovered Syssokans headed him off. He tried to cut back to his right. He slipped in a patch of sand and saved himself from going flat only by catching his weight on both outstretched hands. One of the Syssokans landed across his back, feeling blindly for a hold.

Taranto surged up, trying to butt with the back of his head. He was promptly wrapped in the long arms of another soldier facing him, as the grip from the rear slid down to his waist. The fellow behind him seemed to think he could hurt him by kneading both knobby fists into the spacer's belly, but there was too much hard muscle there.

The Terran again butted, forward this time, and brought up his knee. This was less effective than it should have been, but it helped him free one arm so that he could drive an elbow backward.

The officer ran up with a reversed spear. From the look in his big black eyes, Taranto realized that the Syssokan had also learned something during the melee. That explained, no doubt, why he was an officer. He swung the spear in a neat arc—at Taranto's head!

It cracked against the Terran's skull. Even though he did his best to ride with it, he felt his knees buckle. He struck out with his right fist, but the punch was smothered by the soldier whom he had kneed.

The spear came down again. The world of Taranto's existence was reduced to a narrow view of a straining, greenish-gray calf showing through a torn leg of a Syssokan uniform. Vaguely, he realized that he was on his hands and knees. A

74

great number of hands seemed to be grabbing at him, and his own were very heavy as he groped out for the leg.

He got some sort of fumbling grip, and started to haul himself up. The slowness of his motions alarmed him, in a foggy way. He tried to tuck his chin behind his left shoulder because he knew that there was something . . . something . . . coming . . .

It came. The Syssokan officer's big foot took him behind the ear with a brutal thump.

Taranto, however, sinking into gray nothingness, did not really feel it . . .

ELEVEN

SMITH STOOD AT THE CORNER OF THE CORRIDOR, leaning back every half minute or so to peek around at the stretch leading toward the library and communications room.

Westervelt had propped himself with folded arms against the opposite wall, facing the door to the stairs.

Beryl hovered behind Parrish, who faced Smith impatiently between darting glares at Westervelt.

"All right, I guess I have to tell you, Pete," said Smith in a low tone. "You might say we are temporarily inconvenienced."

"By him?" asked Parrish, jerking a thumb in Westervelt's direction. "That I could understand. The kid's beginning to think he's a comedian. He started out just now playing Charley's Aunt."

"Sssh!" said Smith softly.

Westervelt turned his head toward the main entrance, wondering how far Parrish's voice had carried.

Smith's dapper assistant looked from one to the other. Seeking some evidence of sanity, he turned with raised eyebrows to Beryl. The blonde rounded her blue eyes at him and shrugged.

"Pete, this is no joke," insisted Smith. "I wish it hadn't gotten around so fast, but there it is."

"There *what* is?" demanded Parrish, in a tone bordering on the querulous.

"Well . . . there's been some kind of power failure throughout the business district. There aren't any elevators running, and we don't know how long it will be until the power company copes with the trouble."

"No elevators?" repeated Parrish.

He stared at the sliding doors of the elevator shaft as if unable to comprehend the lack of such service. The idea seemed to sink in.

'No *elevators?* And ninety-nine stories *up?*"

"Sssh!" said Smith, glancing down the corridor.

"What's the matter with you, Castor?" asked Parrish. "Are you watching for someone . . . someone . . . oh!"

"See what I'm thinking?" asked Smith.

They faced each other for a moment in silence.

"Well, it ought to be all right, as long as he can get down the stairs if he wants to," said Parrish. "I'm sorry, Beryl. We'll have to make it some other time."

"But how are we going to get home?" asked the blonde.

"Oh, they'll probably have it fixed by the time we're finished here," said Parrish.

"Then what's all the trouble about. Why is Willie looking so sour?"

Westervelt braced himself against the impact of three glances and tried not to sneer. The other two men cleared their throats and looked back at Beryl.

"I'm going to have to ask your co-operation, Beryl," said Smith. "First, Pete, I'd like to point out to you a little gem of modern design. This door here is powered to slide open automatically for a fire or other emergency."

"Of course," said Parrish curiously.

"But there isn't any power," Smith pointed out.

Parrish reached out impatiently and tried the door. He wrenched at it two or three times, then bent to peer for the latch.

"No use, Pete," said Smith, glancing down the hall again. "Willie already went through that whole routine. I've been on the phone to the building manager, and there isn't anything he can do except send a party up from the seventy-fifth floor to burn open the door from the stair side."

"Is he doing it?"

"Well, frankly . . . I told him it wasn't necessary," said Smith, getting a stubborn look on his long face.

"But you know Bob!" expostulated Parrish. "If he gets the idea that he's penned in here—"

"I know, I know," said Smith. "On the other hand, we can always get something from the lab and break out from this side, provided we take care not to let him know what is going on until later."

Westervelt eyed Beryl sardonically. He had seldom seen an expression so blended of impatience and vague worry. He wondered if anyone would explain to her.

Parris shook his head.

"I think it might be better to call downstairs again, and have them come up," he said.

"I don't want to do that," said Smith.

"Why not?"

"It would get around. Pretty soon, the story would be all over the D.I.R."

Parrish actually leaned forward slightly to study his chief's face. He found no words, but his very expression was plaintive. Smith sighed.

"We're in the business of springing spacers from jails all over the explored galaxy," he said. "We're supposed to be loaded to the jets with high-potency brainwaves and have a gadget for every purpose! How is it going to look if we're locked in our own office and can't get out without help?"

Parrish threw up his hands. Pivoting, he walked loosely a few feet along the corridor and back, squeezing his chin in the palm of one hand. He clasped his hands behind his back, then, and peered around Smith at the empty wing of the corridor.

"Maybe we could dope him," he suggested, without much feeling.

"I should have thought of that," admitted Smith, "but he's finished eating."

"Can't we find something in the lab to shoot a dart?"

As Smith tried to remember, Westervelt interrupted.

"If you decide on that, I'm not volunteering, thank you. Did you ever see Mr. Lydman move in a hurry? Whoever tries it had better not miss with the first dart!"

Smith said, "Harumph!" and Parrish looked uncomfortable. The assistant glanced momentarily at Beryl, but shook his head immediately.

Westervelt followed his thinking. For one thing, Lydman was known to be devoted to his wife and two children; for another, who knew how badly Beryl might miss?

"Now, if everyone will just keep calm," said Smith, "and we can keep Bob busy, we'll probably get along fine until they restore power. How long can it take, after all? They can't waste any time with a large part of a modern city like this cut off. It's unthinkable."

"I suppose you're right," said Parrish.

Smith turned to Beryl.

"What I meant by asking your co-operation," he said, "is that we'll need to have someone with Mr. Lydman most of the time. Willie has been doing it until now, but we don't want it to look like deliberate surveillance."

"But why?" asked Beryl. "I mean . . . I see that it worries

77

all of you that . . . that he might find out. But what if he does?"

"Possibly nothing," answered Smith. "On the other hand, Mr. Lydman was once imprisoned, in his space traveling days. He was held for a long time under very trying conditions; and the experience has left him with a problem. It is not *exactly* claustrophobia. . . ."

He paused, as if to let Beryl recall other remarks about Lydman. Their general air of gravity seemed to impress her.

"I'll be . . . glad to help," she said reluctantly.

"Fine!" said Smith. "Probably nothing will be necessary. Now, I think we had better go in and tell Si, so that everyone will be alerted to the situation."

Westervelt caught the glance that passed between Parrish and Beryl. He was almost certain that each of them was mentally counting the people who had known before *they* had been told.

That's what you get for being so busy in the dead files, he thought.

They trouped in behind Smith. Simonetta watched as if they had been a parade. Smith, with an occasional comment from Parrish, told her the story.

"So that is the partial reason for staying late," he concluded, "although, of course, the case of Harris comes first."

Westervelt had wandered over to a window. He adjusted the filter dial for maximum clarity and looked out.

From where he was, he could see a great black carpet across part of the city, spreading out from somewhere beneath his position until it was cut by a sharp line of street lights many blocks away. Beyond that, the city looked normal. To the near side of the invisible boundary and, he supposed, for a like distance in the opposite direction behind his viewpoint, there were only sparse and faint glows of emergency lights. Some were doubtless powered by buildings with the equipment for the purpose, others were the lights of police and emergency vehicles on the ground or cruising low between the taller buildings.

I wonder what they actually do when something like this happens? he thought. *What if they think they have it fixed, turn on the juice again, and it blows a second time?*

His reverie was interrupted by the sound of Simonetta's phone. From where he was, he could see Joe Rosenkrantz's features as the operator asked for Smith.

"Oh, there you are, Mr. Smith," said Joe. "Pauline has been trying all over. Trident is transmitting, and I thought you would want to be here. They say they have a relay set up right to Harris."

78

Smith let out a whoop and made for the door.

"He'll be right there," Simonetta told the grinning TV man.

Parrish and Westervelt trailed along. When the latter looked back, he saw that Simonetta had replaced Beryl; and he could hardly blame the blonde for seizing the chance to sit down and collect her thoughts. He felt like crawling into a hole somewhere himself.

Passing the library, Parrish cocked an eyebrow at him. Westervelt nodded. He went in and told Lydman about the call. The ex-spacer was interested enough to join the procession.

When Westervelt followed him into the communications room, Joe Rosenkrantz was explaining the set-up to Smith.

"Like before, we go through Pluto, Capella VII, and an automatic relay on an outer planet of the Trident system, but you won't see anything of that. It's after we get Johnson that the fun begins."

He leaned back in his swivel chair before the screen and surveyed the group.

"Johnson is gonna *think* to a fish near his island. This fish thinks to one swimming near Harris. They claim Harris answers."

Smith ran both hands through his hair.

"We try anything," he said. "Let's go!"

Joe got in contact with Johnson, the Terran D.I.R. man, among other things, on Trident. The latter was not quite successful in hiding an I-told-you-so attitude.

"Harris himself confirms that he is being held on the ocean floor," he said. "He seems to be a sort of pet, or curiosity."

"Can you make sense out of the messages?" asked Smith. "I mean, is there any difficulty because of a language barrier? We don't want to make some silly assumption and find out it was based on a misunderstanding."

After the weird pause caused by the mind-numbing distance, Johnson replied.

"There isn't any language barrier in a thought, but you might say there's sometimes an attitude barrier. Uusually, we can pick up an equivalent meaning if we assume, for instance, that our time sense is similar to that of these fish."

"Well, try asking Harris how deep he is," suggested Smith.

They watched Johnson look away, although the man did not seem to be going through any marked effort of concentration. Hardly thirty seconds of this had elapsed when they saw him scowl.

"This fish off my beach can't get it through his massive intellect that he can't think directly to another fish at your position. He thinks you must be pretty queer not to have someone to do your thinking for you."

Smith turned a little red. Westervelt admired Joe Rosen-krantz's pokerface. Johnson appeared to be insisting.

"Harris says he is two minutes' swim under the surface," he reported.

"Well, how far from your position, then?" asked Smith. The distance turned out to be a day-and-a-half swim.

"Does he need anything? Are they keeping him under livable conditions?"

The pause, and Johnson relayed, "They pump him air and feed him. He needs someone to get him out."

"How can we find him?" asked Smith. "Can he work up any way of signaling us?"

"You are signaling him now, he says. He wants you to get him out."

Smith looked around him for questions. Lydman suggested asking how Harris was confined. Smith put it to Johnson, and after the maddening pause, got an answer.

"He says he's in a big glass box like a freight trailer. It's like a cage. Inside, he is free to move around, and he wants to get out."

"Then have him tell us where it is!" snapped Smith.

"He doesn't know," came the reply. "They move about every so often."

"What did I say?" whispered Parrish. "Nomadic."

No one took the time to congratulate him because Smith was asking what the Tridentians were like. Johnson's mental connection seemed to develop static. They saw him shake his head as if to clear it. He turned a puzzled expression to the screen.

"I didn't get that very plainly," he admitted. "A sort of combination of thoughts—they feed him and they don't taste good."

"Well, tell your fishy friend to keep his own opinions out of it," said Smith, surprising Westervelt, who had not quite caught up to the situation.

Johnson, a moment later, grimaced. His expression became apologetic.

"Don't say things like that!" he told Smith, turning again to the screen. "It slipped through my mind as I heard you, and he didn't like it!"

"Who? Harris?"

"No, the fish at his end. I apologized for you."

There was a general restless shifting of feet in the Terran office. Smith seemed, in the dim lighting of the communications room, to flush a deeper shade.

"And what does Harris say?"

Johnson inquired. Harris requested that they get him out.

"Goddammit!" muttered Smith. "He must be punchy!"

"It happens," Lydman reminded him softly.

"Yes," said Smith, after a startled look around, "but some were like that to begin with, and his record suggests it all the way."

He asked Johnson to get a description of the place where Harris found himself. The answer was, in a fashion, conclusive.

"Like any other part of the sea bottom," reported Johnson. "And, furthermore, he's tired of thinking and wants to rest."

"Who does?" demanded Smith.

"They won't tell me," said Johnson, sadly.

Smith choked off a curse, noticing Simonetta standing there. He combed his hair furiously with both hands. No one suggested any other questions, so he thanked Johnson and told Joe to break off.

"At least, we know it's all real," he sighed. "He was actually taken, and he's still alive."

"You put a lot of faith in a couple of fish," said Lydman.

Smith hesitated.

"Well . . . now . . . they aren't really fish," he said. "Let's not build up a mental misconception, just because we've been kidding about 'swishy the thinking fishy.' Actually, they probably wouldn't even suggest fish to an ichthyologist, and they may be a pretty high form of life."

"They may be as high as this Harris," commented Parrish, and earned a cold stare from Lydman.

"I think I'll look around the lab," said the latter, as the others made motions toward breaking up the gathering.

Westervelt promptly headed for the door. He saw that Lydman was walking around the corner of the wire mesh partition that enclosed the special apparatus of the communications room, doubtless bent upon taking a shortcut into the lab.

I want to go sit down a while before they pin me on him again, thought the youth. *I need fifteen minutes, then I'll relieve whoever has him, if Smitty wants me to.*

TWELVE

THE LIGHT, IMPOTENT AFTER PENETRATING FIFTY fathoms of Tridentian sea, was murky and green-tinted; but Tom Harris had become more or less used to that. It rankled, nevertheless, that the sea-people continued to ignore his demands for a lamp.

He knew that they used such devices. Through the clear walls of his tank, he had seen night parties swimming out to hunt small varieties of fish. The water craft they piloted on longer trips and up to the surface were also equipped with lights powered by some sort of battery. It infuriated Harris to be forced arbitrarily to exist isolated in the dimness of the ocean bottom day or the complete blackness of night.

He rose from the spot where he had been squatting on his heels. So smooth was the glassy footing that he slipped and almost fell headlong. He regained his balance and looked about.

The tank was about ten by ten feet and twice as long, with metal angles which he assumed to be aluminum securing all edges. These formed the outer corners, so that he could see the gaskets inside them that made the tank water-tight. The sea-people, he had to admit, were quite capable of coping with their environment and understanding his.

The end of the tank distant from Harris was opaque. He thought that there were connections to a towing vehicle as well as to the plant that pumped air for him. The big fish had not made that quite clear to him. All other sides of the tank were quite clear. Whenever he walked about, he could look through the floor and find groups of shells and other remnants of deceased marine life in the white sand. Occasionally, he considered the pressure that would implode upon him should anything happen to rupture the walls, but he had become habitually successful in forcing that idea to the back of his mind.

Along each of the side walls were four little airlocks. The use of these was at the moment being demonstrated by one of the sea-people to what Harris was beginning to think of as a child.

The parent was slightly smaller than Harris, who stood five-feet-five and weighed a hundred and thirty pounds Terran. It also had four limbs, but that was about the last point they had in common. The Tridentian's limbs all joined his armored body near the head. Two of them ended in powerful pincers; the others forked into several delicate tentacles. The body was somewhat flexible despite the weight of rugged shell segments, and tapered to a spread tail upon which the crustacean balanced himself easily.

Harris felt at a distinct disadvantage in the vision department: each of the Tridentians had four eyes protruding from his chitinous head. The adult had grown one pair of eyestalks to a length of nearly a foot. The second pair, like both of the youngster's, extended only a few inches.

The Terran could not be sure whether the undersea currency consisted of metal or shell, but the Tridentian deposited some sort of coin in a slot machine outside one of the little airlocks. It caused a grinding noise. Directly afterward, a small lump of compressed fish, boned, was ejected from an opening on the inside.

"Goddam' blue lobsters!" swore Harris. "Think they're doing me a favor!"

He let them wait a good five minutes before he decided that the prudent course was to accept the offering. Sneering, he walked over and picked up the food. There was usually little else provided. On days he had been too angry or too disgusted to accept the favors of sightseers, his keepers assumed that he was not hungry.

In the beginning, he had also had a most difficult time getting through to them his need for fresh water. That was when he had come to believe in the large, fish-like swimmer who had transmitted his thoughts to the sea-people. The fact that the latter could and did produce fresh water for him aroused his grudging respect, even though the taste was nothing to take lightly.

He juggled the lump of fish in one hand, causing the little Tridentian to twirl his eye-stalks in glee and swim up off the ocean bottom to look down through the top of the tank. The parent also wiggled his eye-stalks, more sedately. Harris suspected them of laughing, and turned his back.

Looking through the other side of his tank, he could see—to such distance as the murky light permitted—the parked vehicles of the Tridentians. Like a collection of small boats, they were of sundry sizes and shapes, depending perhaps upon each owner's fancy, perhaps on his skill. Harris did not know whether the Tridentians' craftsmanship extended to the level of having professional builders. At any rate, they were spread out like a small city. Among them were tent-like arrangements of nets to keep out swimming vermin. Other than that, the sea-people used no shelters.

They were smart enough to build a cage for me! he thought bitterly. *What the hell is the matter with the Terran government, anyway? That Department of Interstellar Relations, or whatever they call it. Why can't they get me out of here? And where did Big Fish go now?*

He saw several of the crustacean people approaching from the camping area. Shortly, no doubt, he would again be a center of mass attention, with cubes of compressed and stinking fish shooting at him from all the little airlocks. He snarled wordlessly.

The groups seemed to come at certain periods which he had been unable to define. He could only guess that they had choice times for hunting besides other work that had to be done to maintain the campsite and their jet-propelled craft.

I'd like to get one of them in here and boil him! thought Harris. *Big Fish claims they don't taste good. I wonder. Anyway, it would shake them up!*

He had long since given up thinking about what the sea-people could do to him if they chose. Their flushing the tank eighteen inches deep with sea water twice a day had soon given him an idea, especially as he had nowhere to go during the process. He no longer permitted himself to fall asleep anywhere near the inlet pipe.

He noticed that the dozen or so sightseers were edging around the end of the tank to join the first individual and his offspring. Looking up, Harris saw the reason. A long, dark shadow was curving down in an insolently deliberate dive. It was streamlined as a Terran shark and as long as the tank in which Harris lived. The flat line of its leading edge split into something very like a yawn, displaying astonishing upper and lower carpets of conical teeth. This was possible because the eyes, about eight Harris thought, were spaced in a ring about the head end of the long body.

They know I don't like to eat them, but I like to scare them a little. Big Fish thought to Harris. *Look at them trying to smile at me!*

Harris watched the Tridentians wiggling and waving their eye-stalks as the monster passed lazily over them and turned to come slowly back.

"I'd like to scare them a lot," said Harris, who had learned some time ago that he got through better just by forgetting telepathy and verbalizing. "Is the D.I.R. man still there?"

Which . . . what you thought? inquired Big Fish.

"The other Terran, the one on the island."

The other air-breathing one is gone, the other Big Fish is

84

feeding, as I have done just now, and it is not clear about the far Terran who lacks a Big Fish.

"All the bastards on both worlds are out to lunch," growled Harris, "and here I sit!"

You are in to lunch, agreed the monster.

The three eyes that bore upon the imprisoned man as the thinker swept past the tank had an intelligent alertness. Harris had come to imagine that he could detect expressions on Big Fish's limited features.

"You're the only friend I've got!" he exclaimed, slipping suddenly into self-pity. "I wish I could go with you."

Once you could, when you had your own tank.

"It was what we call a submarine," said Harris. "I was looking to see what was on the ocean floor. Tell me, is it all like this?"

Is it all like what? With blue lobsters?

Harris still retained enough sanity to realize that the Tridentians did not suggest Terran lobsters to this being who probably could not even imagine them. That was an automatic translation of thought furnished out of his own memory and name-calling.

"No," he said. "I mean is it all sand and mud with a few chasms here and there? Where do these crabs get their metals?"

There are different kinds of holes and hills. It is all mostly the same. You cannot swim in it anywhere, although there are little things that dig under the soft sand. Some of them are good to eat but you have to spit out a lot of sand. The crabs dig with machines sometimes, in big holes, but what they catch I do not know.

"Isn't there anything that catches *them?*" asked Harris bitterly.

No. They are big enough to catch other things, except a few. Things that are bigger than I am are not smart.

The monster made a pass along the ocean bed near the Tridentians, stirring up a cloud of sand and causing Harris's captor to shrink against the side of his tank. The Terran laughed heartily. He clapped the backs of his fists against his forehead above the eyes and wiggled his forefingers at the Tridentians on the other side of the clear barrier.

Even after the sand had settled, he ran back and forth along the side of his tank, making sure that every sightseer had opportunity to note his gesture. He had an idea that they did not like it much.

They do not like it at all, thought Big Fish. *Some of them are asking for the man who lets the sea into your tank.*

"Don't call it a man!" objected Harris, giving up his posturing. "I am a man."

What else can I call these men except men? asked the other. *I do not understand why you want to be called a man. You are different.*

"Forget it," said Harris. "It was just a figure of thought."

He felt like sitting down again, but decided against it in case the onlookers should succeed in obtaining the services of the tank attendant. He walked to the end of the tank, where he could stare into the greenish distance without looking at the Tridentian camp.

"I wish I were dead," he muttered. "They'll never get me out of here."

Behind him, he heard the plop-plop of food tidbits landing on the floor of the tank as the onlookers sought to regain his attention. They must have come out of their moment of pique if they were trying to coax him to amuse them further.

"If I could find a bone in those hunks of fish, I'd kill myself," said Harris.

The dark shape of Big Fish settled over the tank, cutting off what little light there was like a cloud. Harris looked up resentfully.

I do not understand you, thought the monster. *That would be very foolish.*

"What—trying to commit suicide with a fish bone?"

No matter how, it would be extremely foolish, for then you would be dead.

Harris could not think of anything to say. He could not even think of anything to think, obviously, since none of his chaotic, half-formed thoughts brought a response.

It would be as if you had been eaten, insisted his friend.

"All right, all right! I won't do it then, if that'll make you happy," exclaimed Harris.

It has no effect on how well I feed, Big Fish informed him.

It took Harris a minute, but he figured it out.

"So that's your philosophy!" he muttered to himself. "Now I know what it takes to make you happy. Something to eat!"

Where? inquired the monster. *I do not see anyone I want to eat.*

"Never mind!" said Harris. "Tell me more about the ocean bottom. Where there are big holes or cliffs, can you see . . . uh . . . stripes in the sides, layers of rock?"

Sometimes. Where it is deep enough. Other places there are things growing to the bottom. Only little fish that are not even good to eat do their feeding there. Sometimes the sea-people take away the growing things or dig holes.

"I'll bet there are plenty of things to get out of this

86

ocean," mused Harris. "Who knows how the climate may have changed in thousands of years. Maybe if there was an ice age the seas would have shrunk. Maybe there was a volcanic age. Maybe you could drill underwater and find oil—if you knew where to look. Maybe there are deposits of diamonds under the ooze."

He stopped when he sensed a vague irritation. He realized that his thoughts had been going out and scoring the cleanest of misses.

"It doesn't matter," he said. "Just tell me what you do know about the sea."

I can tell you where to find tribes of the sea-people. I can tell you where to find all sorts of good eating-fish. I know where to think to other Big Fish but that I cannot tell you, for you cannot feel it.

The monster rose slowly through the water. He had seen something up there that interested him, Harris knew, and would return when it occurred to him.

He considered the possibilities. Perhaps there was something in the idea of building up a food industry. If you had inside tips on where the fish were, how could you miss? Then, the Tridentians must have some knowledge of where to find metals, since they used them. He suspected that they had factories somewhere.

"Come to think of it," he asked himself, "how do I know it isn't some savage tribe that picked me up? One of these days, I may wind up with a more advanced bunch. I'll have to ask Big Fish when he comes back."

He began to plan what he would do if he reached some higher civilization under the sea. Anyone with the knowledge to mine metals, or maybe to extract them from sea water, would be interested in contacting Terrans from another world. There would be a little trouble, probably, in getting them to comprehend space, but some of them could be sent up to the surface in tanks. Then there would be a need for some Terran who knew both worlds.

"I could wind up an ambassador!" Harris told himself. "I wonder . . . maybe I could even work it with this bunch. If I could only get out of here! Come back in another submarine, maybe."

He began to pace the length of his tank and back, stopping once to gather up the fish that had been bought for him by some of the crowd outside. He noted that the latter was constantly changing without varying much in total number. He took to walking around the sides of the tank, staring into each set of eyes.

In the end, this had such a hypnotic effect that he imagined himself swimming through the dim, greenish light. The sea-people outside began to appear as individuals. He grew into the feeling that he could recognize one from the other.

He found himself running for the corner where he had collected his fish. The sound that had triggered the reaction originated at the opaque end of the tank. It was followed within seconds by several jets of water, white and forceful, which entered near the floor of the structure.

Harris snatched up his supply of food to keep it from being washed away. With one hand, he tried to roll up the legs of his pants. He never seemed to be prepared when the time came, but he was constantly too chilled to go around with the trousers rolled up all the time.

The water swished about the calves of his legs. After a few minutes, it began to recede as the Tridentian machinery pumped it out. Soon, the tank was clean of everything but Harris, his fish, and the thick smell of sea water.

He was good, came a thought. *I see you are eating too.*

A large shadow passed overhead. Most of the Tridentians wiggled their eye-stalks in an effort to look amiable. Harris dropped his fish to the damp floor.

"No, I'm not eating," he said. "I'm all wet."

So am I, answered Big Fish.

"But I'm not usually," said Harris.

I know. It is unkind, they way they let you dry out. Would you like me to knock in the end of the tank? You could have all the water you want.

"Not right now," said Harris calmly. He sat down, crossing his legs. "I'll have to grow some gills first. It may not take much longer, at that."

He looked at the Tridentians, who looked in at him. Again, he felt the sensation of being able to recognize individuals. Perhaps he should talk to them more often through Big Fish.

"Maybe some of them are really nice fellows," he muttered, "if I just get to know them better."

No, his friend told him, *they are not very good to eat.*

THIRTEEN

TIME HAD DRAGGED ITS SLOW WAY PAST SIX-thirty. The excuse of a flying start on the Harris case had worn thin to the point of delicacy—to all but one man. The rest of them hoped sincerely that *he* was keeping himself interested.

Westervelt sat at his desk, perusing an article in *Spaceman's World* about the exploration of a newly discovered planetary system. It might come up in a conference someday, he reflected, and it might be as well to know a few facts on the subject. No life had been discovered on any of the dozen planets, but that did not necessarily preclude the establishment of a Terran colony in the future. The department also had problems with colonies, as witness Greenhaven.

He put down the magazine for a moment to review the personnel situation.

Parrish, he remembered, had expressed his intention of retreating to his office and putting in an hour or two of desk-heeling. Under the circumstances, he had declared, there was little point in digging further into the files for an idea since that was not at all their primary purpose in staying late. Rosenkrantz, of course, was on watch in the communications room. Smith wandered in and out. Simonetta had taken a portable taper down to Lydman's office to help organize a preliminary report the chief had requested from him. After she had returned, and fallen to low-voiced gossip through the window with Pauline, Beryl had been sent back with a number of scribbled objections for Lydman to answer.

Smith had spent all of five minutes thinking them up—before Simonetta brought the original report. Westervelt wondered how soon Beryl would return with the answers, because it would then probably be his turn to ride herd.

He did not regard the idea with relish.

Smith strolled out of his office. He halted to survey the nearly empty office with an air of vague surprise, then saw Simonetta outside Pauline's cubicle. He went over to join the conversation.

I should have walked out somewhere, thought Westervelt. *Now the door is completely blockaded.*

The magazine article turned dull immediately.

Sure enough, in a few minutes Smith approached Westervelt's corner.

"Who's on watch, Willie?" he asked, attempting a jovial wink.

"Beryl, I think," answered the youth. "Must be—she hasn't been around."

"She's been there quite a while," commented Smith. "I have a feeling that it's time for a shift. How about wandering down there and edging in?"

"What would I say?" objected Westervelt. "He's probably dictating his remarks and wouldn't like me hanging around."

89

Smith chewed on his lower lip.

"For the questions I sent him," he muttered thoughtfully, "five minutes should have been enough. Goldilocks has been with him over half an hour."

"But he must be tired of my face," said Westervelt.

"I don't have anyone else to send, unless you want me to think up an excuse for Pauline. Asking him to help with her homework would be pretty thin."

Westervelt thought it over. Parrish, in his present mood, was not likely to be of any help. Simonetta had just done her stint, and Joe was needed on the space set. It would have been nice if there were a message for Lydman to listen to, but that was wishful dreaming.

"All right, Mr. Smith," he surrendered. "Maybe I can take along this article and ask if he's seen it yet. If he's taking an inventory or trying out something in the lab, I'll take my life in my hands and volunteer to help!"

Smith laughed.

"It can't be that bad, Willie," he said, slapping the other on the shoulder.

Westervelt was not so sure, but he folded the magazine open to the beginning of his article and went out. Pauline peered at him as he passed.

"Don't look like that!" he said. "You'll see me again, I hope!"

"You might try looking a little more confident of that yourself," Simonetta called after him.

Westervelt turned the corner and walked slowly down the hall, trying out more confident expressions as he went. None of them felt exactly right.

Passing the spare office where the dead files were kept, he heard a sound.

They must have come up here for something, he thought. *That's why it seemed so long to Smitty.*

He had opened the door and taken one step inside before he realized that the room was dark. Without thinking, he reached out to flip the light switch.

Beryl Austin leaped to her feet with a flash of thigh that hardly registered on Westervelt in the split-second of his astonishment. Then he saw that she had not been alone on the settee that stood beside the door. Parrish rose beside her.

The suddenness of their movements and the ferocity of their combined stares had the impact of a stunning blow upon Westervelt. The implications of the blonde's slightly disheveled appearance, however, were obvious.

He could not, for a moment, think at all. Then he began to have a feeling that he ought to say something to cover his escape. Beneath that, somewhere, surged the conviction

90

that he had nothing to apologize for. In the face of such hostility and tension, it called for a lot of courage.

"You little sneak!" spat Beryl.

Westervelt noted with a certain detachment that her voice had turned shrill. Not knowing of anything else to do, he stared as she tugged her dress into place. This seemed to outrage her more than anything he could have said. He also saw the gleam of Parrish's teeth, and the grimace was not even remotely a smile. The man took a step to place himself before Beryl.

"What do you think you're doing?" demanded Parrish, with a good deal more feeling than originality.

Westervelt had been wondering what to say to that when it came, as was inevitable. A dozen half-expressed answers flitted through his mind.

How do you get out of a thing like this? he asked himself desperately. *You'd think it was me that did it!*

Before he could explore the implications of his choosing the words "did it," Beryl found her voice again.

"Get out of here!" she shrilled. "Who told you to come poking in?"

"I heard a noise," said Westervelt, conscious that his voice sounded odd. "I thought it was Mr. Lydman."

"Do I look like Lydman?" demanded Parrish, not raising his voice as much as Beryl had. "There wasn't any light, was there? Did you think he'd be sitting in here in the dark?"

The possibility charged the atmosphere like static electricity. Actually, mere mention of it made Westervelt feel better because it sounded so much like what he might have found.

"How did I know?" he retorted. "I thought Beryl was with him. Why should I expect *you?* You said you weren't going to dig any further in here."

Beryl had been smoothing her still-perfect coiffure. Now she stiffened as much as Parrish. Westervelt sensed that his choice of words might have been unfortunate.

"Well, who *is* with him?" he demanded, before they could say anything.

The question galvanized Parrish into action. He stepped forward to meet Westervelt face to face.

"If you're so worried about that, why don't you go find him?" he sneered. "For my money, you two make a good match."

"Maybe I will," said Westervelt hotly. "*You* two don't seem to care about what's going on. If you'll just excuse me, I'll turn out the light and—"

"Oh, cut out the speech-making!" requested Beryl. "Get out

of the door, Willie, and let me out of here. I'm tired of the whole incident."

"Now, wait a minute, Beryl!" protested Parrish.

"Yeah," said Westervelt, "you'd better check. Your lipstick is really smudged this time."

"Shut up, you!" Parrish snapped.

He took Beryl by the shoulders and pulled her back. She pulled herself free peevishly. Westervelt leaned against the wall and curled a lip.

"Enough is enough!" she said. "Let me out of here!"

"You forgot to smile," Westervelt told Parrish.

The man turned on him and reached out to seize a handful of his shirtfront. Westervelt straightened up, alarmed but willing to consider changing the smooth mask of Parrish's face. Beryl was shrilling something about not being damned fools, when she stopped in the middle of a word.

Parrish also grew still. The forearm Westervelt had crossed over the hand grabbing at his shirt fell as Parrish let him go. The man was staring over Westervelt's shoulder. He looked almost frightened.

Westervelt looked around—and a thrill shot through him, like the shock of diving into icy water.

Lydman was standing there, staring through him.

When he looked again, as he shrank instinctively away from the doorway, he realized that the ex-spacer was staring through all of them. After a moment, he seemed to focus on Beryl.

"They'll let you out, I think," he said in his quiet voice.

Parrish stepped back nervously, and Westervelt edged further inside the doorway to make room. Beryl did not seem to have heard. She gaped, hypnotized by the beautiful eyes set in the strong, tanned face.

Lydman put the palm of one hand against Westervelt's chest and shoved slowly. It was as well that the file cabinet behind the youth was nearly empty, because it slid a foot along the floor as his back flattened against it. Lydman reached out his other hand and took Beryl gently by the elbow.

She stepped forward, turning her head from side to side as if to seek reassurance from either Parrish or Westervelt, but without completely meeting their eyes. Lydman led her into the hall and released her elbow.

She started uncertainly up the corridor toward the main office. Lydman fell in a pace or two behind her.

Westervelt heard a gasp. He looked at Parrish and realized that he had been holding his breath too. Then, by mutual consent, they followed the others out into the hall.

"Listen, Willie," whispered Parrish, watching the twenty-foot gap between them and Lydman's broad shoulders, "we

92

have to see that she doesn't forget and try to leave. If he won't let me talk to her, you'll have to get her attention."

"Okay, I'll try," murmured Westervelt. "Look—I was really looking for him. I never meant to—"

"I never meant to either," said Parrish. "Forget it!"

"It was none of my business. I should have shut up and left. Tell her I'm sorry when you get a chance; she'll probably never speak to me again."

He wondered if he could get Smith's permission to move his desk. On second thought, he wondered if he would come out of this with a desk to move.

"Sure she will," said Parrish. "She's really just a good-natured kid. It wasn't anything serious. You startled us, that was all."

Beryl and Lydman turned the corner, leaving the two followers free to increase their pace. They rounded the corner themselves in time to see Lydman going through the double doors.

"It was too bad he came along when she was yelling to be let out," said Parrish. "He didn't understand."

"You mean he actually thought we were trying to keep her there against her will?" asked Westervelt.

"Well, we were, I suppose, or at least I was. He doesn't seem to think any further than that in such situations. If someone is being held against his will, that's enough for Bob. Did you know Smitty had to post a bond for him?"

"A bond!" repeated Westervelt. "What for?"

"They caught him a couple of times, trying out his new gadgets around the city jail. I'll tell you about it sometime."

Parrish fell silent as they reached the entrance to the main office. Beryl had gratefully stopped to speak to the first person in sight, which happened to be Pauline. As Parrish and Westervelt arrived, she was offering to take over the switchboard for twenty minutes or so.

"Oh, I didn't mean you had to drop everything," Pauline was protesting. "I just meant . . . when you get the chance . . ."

She eyed Lydman curiously, then looked to the late arrivals. The silly thought that Joe Rosenkrantz must feel awfully lonely crossed Westervelt's mind, and he had to fight down a giggle.

"You really should get out of there for a while," advised Lydman, studying the size of Pauline's cubbyhole. "Sit outside a quarter of an hour at least, and let your mind spread out."

"Well, if it's really all right with you, Beryl?"

"I'm only too glad to help," said Beryl rapidly.

93

She wasted no time in rounding the corner to get at the door. Westervelt closed his eyes. He found it easy to envision Pauline tangling with her on the way out and causing Lydman to start all over again.

The girls managed without any such catastrophe. Pauline headed for the swivel chair behind the unused secretarial desk.

"You ought to leave that door open," Lydman called to Beryl. "If it should stick, there's hardly any air in there. You'd feel awfully cramped in no time."

"Thank you," said Beryl politely.

She left the door open, sat down, and picked up Pauline's headset. From the set of her shoulders, it did not seem that much light conversation would be forthcoming from that quarter.

Westervelt stepped further into the office, and saw that Smith was standing in his own doorway, rubbing his large nose thoughtfully. The youth guessed that Simonetta had signalled him.

Parrish cleared his throat with a little cough.

"Well," he said, "I'll be in my office if anyone wants me."

Rather than pass too close to Lydman, he retreated into the hall to use the outside entrance to his office. The ex-spacer paid no attention.

Westervelt decided that he would be damned if he would go through Parrish's office and back into this one to get at his desk. He walked around the projection of the switchboard cubicle and sat down with a sigh at his own place. He leaned back and looked about, to discover that Lydman had gone over to say a few words to Smith. Pauline glanced curiously from Westervelt to the two men, then began to shop among a shelf of magazines beside the desk of the vacationing secretary.

After a few minutes, Lydman turned and went out the door. Westervelt tried to listen for footsteps, but the resilient flooring prevented him from guessing which way the ex-spacer had gone.

He saw Smith approaching, and went to meet him.

"I've changed my mind," said the chief. "For a little bit, anyway, we'll leave him alone. He said he was sketching up some gizmo he wants to have built, and needed peace and quiet."

"Did he say we . . . were talking too loud?" asked Westervelt, looking at the doorway rather than meet Smith's eye.

"No, that was all he said," answered Smith.

There was a questioning undertone in his voice, but Westervelt chose not to hear it. After a short wait, Smith asked

Simonetta to bring her taper into his office. He mentioned that he hoped to phone for some technical information. Westervelt watched them leave, then sank down on the corner of the desk at which Pauline was relaxing.

Beryl turned around in her chair.

"Pssst! Pauline!" she whispered. "Is he gone?"

"They all left—except Willie," the girl told her.

Beryl shut the door promptly. The pair left in the office heard her turn the lock with a brisk snap.

"What's the matter with her?" murmured Pauline.

"Nothing," said Westervelt glumly. "Why don't you take a nap, or something?"

"I'd like to," said Pauline. "It's going on seven o'clock and who knows when we'll get out of here?"

"Shut up!" said Westervelt. "I mean . . . uh . . . don't bring us bad luck by talking about it. Take a nap and let me think."

"All you big thinkers!" jeered Pauline. "What I'd really like to do is go down to the ladies' room and take a shower, but you always kid me about Mr. Parrish maybe coming in with fresh towels for the machine."

"I lied to you, Pauline," said Westervelt. "The charwoman brings them."

"Well, I could always hope," giggled Pauline.

"Not tonight," said Westervelt. "Believe me, kid, you're safer than you'll ever be!"

FOURTEEN

PAULINE CAME BACK IN A QUARTER OF AN HOUR, her youthfully translucent skin glowing and her ash-blonde curls rearranged. She glanced through the window at Beryl, who was nervously punching a number for an outside call.

"What's going on?" she asked Westervelt, who sat with his heels on the center desk.

"Mr. Smith is calling a couple of engineers he knows," Simonetta told her.

Westervelt had just heard it, when Simonetta had emerged with a tape to transcribe. He had started to mention that it might be better to phone a psychiatrist, but had bitten back the remark.

95

For all I know, he reflected, *they might take me away! Everything I remember about today can't really have happened. If it did, I wish it hadn't!*

He recalled that he had been phoned at home to hop a jet for London that morning. He had found the laboratory which had made the model of the light Smith was interested in, and been on his way back without time for lunch. Now that the jets were so fast, meals were no longer served on them, and he had had to grab a sandwich upon returning. Then there had been those poor fried eggs. That was all—no wonder he was feeling hungry again!

I should have missed the return jet, he thought bitterly. *I didn't know where I was well off! Why did I have to walk in there? I might have had the sense to go look in Bob's office first.*

He decided that Pauline, now chatting with Simonetta, looked refreshed and relaxed. Perhaps he ought to do the same.

The idea, upon reflection, continued to appear attractive. Westervelt rose and walked out past the switchboard. Beryl was too busy to see him. He made his way quietly to the rest room, which he found empty. He was rather relieved to have avoided everyone.

At one side of the room was a door leading to a shower. The appointments of Department 99 were at least as complete as those of any modern business office of the day. Westervelt stepped into a tiny anteroom furnished with a skimpy stool, several hooks on the wall, and a built-in towel supplier.

Prudently, he set the temperature for a hot shower on the dial outside the shower compartment, and punched the button that turned on the water.

Just in case all the trouble has affected the hot water supply, he thought.

As he undressed, he was reassured by the sight of steam inside the stall. Another thought struck him. He locked the outer door. He did not care for the possibility of having Lydman imagine that he was trapped in here. It would be just his luck to be "assisted" out into the corridor, naked and dripping, at the precise moment it was full of staff members on their way to the laboratory.

He slid back the partly opaqued plastic doors and stepped with a sigh of pleasure under the hot stream. Ten minutes of it relaxed him to the point of feeling almost at peace with the world once more.

"I ought to finish with a minute or two of cold," he told himself, "but to hell with it! I'll set the air on cool later."

He pushed the waterproof button on the inside of the stall to turn off the water, opened the narrow doors, and reached out to the towel dispenser. The towel he got was fluffy and large, though made of paper. He blotted himself off well before turning on the air jets in the stall to complete the drying process.

Having dressed and disposed of the towel through a slot in the wall, he glanced about to see if he had forgotten anything. The shower stall had automatically aired itself, sucking all moisture into the air-conditioning system; and looked as untouched as it had at his entrance.

Westervelt strolled out into the rest room proper, thankful that the lock on the anteroom door had not chosen that moment to stick. He stretched and yawned comfortably. Then he caught sight of his tousled, air-blown hair in a mirror. He fished in his pocket for coins and bought another hard paper comb and a small vial of hair dressing from dispensers mounted on the wall. He took his time spraying the vaguely perfumed mist over his dark hair and combing it neatly.

That task attended to, he stole a few seconds to study the reflection of his face. It was rather more square about the jaw than Smith's, he thought, but he had to admit that the nose was prominent enough to challenge the chief's. No one had thought to equip the washroom with adjustable mirrors, so he gave up twisting his neck in an effort to see his profile.

"Well, that's a lot better!" he said, with considerable satisfaction. "Now if I can hook another coffee out of the locker, it will be like starting a new day. Gosh, I hope it's a better one, too!"

He walked lightly along the corridor to the main office, exaggerating the slight resilience of the floor to a definite bounce in his step. Outside the office, he met Beryl coming out. He felt himself come down on his heels immediately.

Beryl eyed him enigmatically, glanced over his shoulder to check that he was alone, and swung away toward the opposite wing. Westervelt hurried after her.

"Look, Beryl!" he called. "I wanted to say . . . that is . . . about before—"

Beryl turned the corner and kept walking.

"Wait just a second!" said Westervelt.

He tried to get beside her to speak to something besides the back of her blonde head, but she was a tall girl and had a long stride. He hesitated to take her by the elbow.

Beryl stopped at the door to the library.

"Please take note, Willie," she said coldly, "that the light is on inside and I am all alone."

97

At least she spoke, thought Westervelt.

"I have come down here for a little peace and quiet," she informed him. "I hope you didn't intend to learn how to read at this hour of the night."

"Aw, come on!" protested Westervelt. "It was an accident. Could I help it?"

"Being the way you are, I suppose not," admitted Beryl judiciously. "Why don't you go elsewhere and be an accident again?"

"I'm trying to say I'm sorry," said Westervelt, feeling a flush spreading over his features. "I don't know why I have to apologize, anyway. It wasn't *me* in there, filing away in the dark!"

Beryl looked down her nose at him as if he were a Mizarian asking where he could have his chlorine tank refilled.

"Is that the story you're telling around?" she demanded icily.

"I'm not telling—" Westervelt realized he was beginning to yell, and lowered his voice. "I'm not telling any story around. Nobody knows anything about it except you and I and Pete. Bob couldn't have seen anything."

Beryl shrugged, a small, disdainful gesture. Westervelt wondered why he had allowed himself to get into an argument over the matter, since it was obvious that he was making things worse with every word.

"I don't know why you should be so sore about it," he said. "Even Pete said to me I should forget about it."

"Oh, you two have been talking it over!" Beryl accused. "Pretty clubby! Do you take over for him on other things too?"

Westervelt threw up his hands.

"You don't seem to mind anything about it except that I should know you were in there with him," he retorted. "If he was so acceptable, why am I a disease? Nobody ever left this office on account of me!"

"It could happen yet," said Beryl.

"Oh, hell! The trouble with you is you need a little loosening up."

He grabbed her by the shoulders and yanked her toward him. Slipping his left arm behind her back as she tried to kick his ankle, he kissed her. The result was spoiled by Beryl's turning her face away at the crucial instant. Westervelt drew back.

The next thing he knew, lights exploded before his right eye. He had not even seen her hand come up, or he would have ducked. He saw it as he stepped back, however. Despite a certain feminine delicacy, the hand clenched into a very capable little fist.

98

Beryl took one quick stride into the library.

"I don't like to keep hinting around," she said, "but maybe that will play itself back in your little mind."

She slammed the door three inches from his nose. Westervelt raised a hand to open it, then changed his mind and felt gingerly of his eye. It hurt, but with a sort of surrounding numbness.

Realizing that he could see after all, he looked up and down the corridor guiltily. It seemed very quiet.

Right square in the peeper! he thought ruefully. *She couldn't have aimed that well: it must have been a lucky shot. I ought to go in there and belt her!*

It was not something he really wanted to do. He could not foresee any pleasure or satisfaction in carrying matters to the extent of open war.

You lost again, Willie, he argued. *You might as well take it like a man. She got annoyed at something you said, like as not, and it was too late when you began.*

He prodded gently at his eye again, and decided that the numb sensation was being caused by the tightening of skin over a growing mouse.

He set off up the corridor, passed the main door with his face averted, and hurried down to the washroom before someone should come along.

Spying out the land through a cautiously opened door, he discovered the place unoccupied. In the mirror, the eye showed definite signs of blossoming. The eyebrow was all right, but the orb itself was bloodshot and tearing freely. Beneath it, the flesh above the cheekbone was pink and puffy.

"Ohmigod!" breathed Westervelt. "It'll be blue tomorrow! Probably purple and green, in fact. Or does it take a day or two to reach that stage?"

He ran cold water into a basin and splashed it over his face, holding a palmful at a time against the damaged eye.

When this did not seem sufficiently effective, he wadded a soft paper towel, soaked it in running water, and applied it until it lost its chill.

"Am I doing right?" he wondered. "I can never remember whether it's hot or cold you're supposed to use."

He thought about it while holding the slowly disintegrating towel to his eye. Someone had told him, as nearly as he could recall, that either way helped, depending upon when heat or cold was applied.

"I guess it must be that you use cold before it has, time to swell," he muttered. "Keep the blood from going into the tissues—that must be it. But if you're too late for that, then

99

heat would keep it from stiffening. Now, the question is, did I start in time?"

He examined the eye. It did not feel too sore, but it was still red and slightly swollen. The flow of tears had stopped, so he decided there was little more he could do. He dried his face and walked out into the corridor, blinking.

The com room is pretty dim, he thought.

He went to the laboratory door and opened it quietly. The room was dark and unoccupied. Westervelt swore to himself that if he stumbled over anyone this time, he would punch every nose he could reach without further ado. Unless, he amended the intention, he ran into Lydman.

He was squeamish about turning on a light, which left him the problem of groping his way through the maze of tables, workbenches, and stacks of cartons. He set down for future conversation the possibility of claiming that the department was as normal as any other business; it too possensed the typical, messy back room out of range of the front office.

He had negotiated about half the course when he felt a cool breeze. At first, he thought it must come from an air-conditioning diffuser, but it blew more horizontally. Someone must have opened a window, he decided, or perhaps broken one trying out a dangerous instrument.

He succeeded in reaching the far wall, where he felt around for the door leading to the communications room. This was over near the outside wall, but he reached it without bumping into more than two or three scattered objects.

Once through the door, he could see better because a little light was diffused past the wire-mesh enclosure around the power equipment. He walked along the short passage formed by this, turned a corner, and came in sight of Joe Rosenkrantz sitting before his screen.

"Hello, Joe," he greeted the operator.

The other jumped perceptibly, looking around at the door.

"It's Willie," said Westervelt. "I came around the other way."

He was pleased to find that Rosenkrantz had the room as dimly lighted as was customary among the TV men. Joe stared for a moment at him and Westervelt feared that the other's vision was too well adjusted to the light.

"I didn't think anybody but Lydman used that way much," said Rosenkrantz.

"It's a short-cut," said Westervelt evasively.

He found a spare chair to sit in and inquired as to what might be new.

Rosenkrantz told him of putting through a few calls to

planets near Trident, asking D.I.R. men stationed on them to line up spaceships for possible use, either to go after Harris or to ship necessary equipment for plumbing the ocean. He offered to let Westervelt scan the tapes of his traffic.

"That's a good idea," said the youth gratefully. "Even if I don't spot an opening, it will look like useful effort."

"Yeah," agreed the other. "Time drags, doesn't it. Wonder how they're making out down in the cable tunnels?"

"It can't last much longer."

"That's what this here Harris is saying too, I should think. Now, *there's* one guy who is really packed away!"

"Well . . ."

"Oh, they've pulled some good ones around here, but I have a feeling about this one," insisted the operator. "I'd bet ten to one they won't spring Harris."

Westervelt took the tapes to a playback screen and dragged his chair over.

"I told Smitty they ought to offer to swap for him," he said. "At the time, I meant it looked like the perfect way to unload undesirables. Come to think of it, though, I wouldn't mind going myself."

"What the hell for?" asked Rosenkrantz.

Westervelt realized that he had nearly given himself away.

"Oh . . . just for the chance to see the place," he said. "Nobody else has ever seen these Tridentians. How else could somebody like me get a position as an interstellar ambassador."

"Maybe Harris wants the job for himself. He sure went looking for it!"

The phone buzzed quietly. Rosenkrantz answered, then said, "It's for you."

Westervelt went to the screen. It was Smith.

"I thought you must have found a way out, Willie. Where did you get to?"

Westervelt explained that he was looking at the tapes of the Trident calls, to familiarize himself with the background.

"I figured there was plenty of time for me to—" He broke off as he saw Rosenkrantz straighten up to focus in a call from space. "Joe is receiving something right now. I'll let you know if it has anything to do with Trident."

"Department 99, Terra," the operator was saying when Westervelt turned from the phone, as if the mere call signal had not satisfied the party at the other end.

There seemed to be a lot of action on the screen. Men were running in various directions in what appeared to be a large hall with an impressive stairway.

"Yoleen!" Rosenkrantz flung over his shoulder. "Tell Smitty!"

"Mr. Smith!" said Westervelt, turning back to the phone screen. "Joe says it's Yoleen coming in. Maybe you'd like to see it yourself. Something looks wrong."

"Coming!" said Smith, and the phone went dark.

Westervelt looked around to see that most of the running figures had hidden themselves. A voice was coming over, and he listened with the operator.

". . . knocked apart so I have to use one of the observation lenses they have planted around the embassy. He's shooting up the place good!"

"I'm taping until someone gets here," said Rosenkrantz. "Better tell me what happened, just in case."

Yoleen, thought Westervelt. *That would be . . . let me see . . . Gerson, the kidnap case. Do they mean that he's shooting them up?*

". . . and after he left me with this mess in the com room, he headed for the stairs," said the voice of the unseen operator. "He seems to be trying to get out of the embassy. We don't know why—the boys got him there without any trouble."

"Was he all right?" asked Rosenkrantz, cocking an ear at the door.

"He looked pretty sick, as if he wasn't eating well, and he had a broken wrist. They took him along to the doctor with no trouble. Then the chief went up to see how he was and found Doc out cold on the floor. He set up a yell, naturally. Someone finally caught up with Gerson in the military attache's office."

"What did he want there?" asked Rosenkrantz.

"We don't know yet. He left a corpse for us that isn't answering questions."

FIFTEEN

IN THE BUILDING TO WHICH THE TWO TERRANS had brought him, Gerson crouched behind the ornate balustrade edging the mezzanine. He was near the head of the stairway and hoped to get nearer.

A look down the hall behind him showed no unwary heads

in view. He studied the sections of the hall below, which he could see through the openings in the railing. There had been a great scrambling about down there a moment earlier, so he was uneasy about showing himself.

He had armed himself as chance provided: a rocket pistol of Yoleenite manufacture—doubtless purchased as a souvenir—and a sharp knife from a dinner tray he had come upon in one of the rooms he had searched. Because of his injury, he had to grip the knife between his teeth. Something bothered him about this arrangement. He had the papers thrust in his shirt, he held the rocket pistol in one hand, one hand was hurt—yet the only way left to hold the knife was in his teeth. It did not seem exactly right, but he had had no time to ponder. The Terrans were keeping him busy.

Since he had been brought to this building, he had seen four threes of Terrans. One, the medical worker, he had rendered helpless. Then he had gone to search for secrets, and that other one had seen him. By that time, he had found the rocket pistol. He had left that Terran dead, but others had come running.

Something had told him to shoot up the communications equipment, although the Terran working it had escaped. He was somewhere behind Gerson, behind one of the many doors leading off that high, bright corridor.

He believed that he had seen one other duck into a doorway ahead of him, along the hall on the other side of the mezzanine. There was yet another hiding behind the opposite balustrade. Gerson wondered idly if the last one was armed.

He tried to review the probable positions of those on the main floor. One had definitely run out the front door, which faced the bottom of the broad stairway, about thirty feet away. There was a shallow anteroom there, but Gerson had seen him all the way across it.

Of the others, one had ducked into a chamber at the front of the main hall, to Gerson's left as he would be descending the stairs. Another had run back under cover of the stairway on the same side, and the remaining four were lurking somewhere to the right, either behind the stairs or in adjoining chambers.

He leaned closer to the balustrade in an effort to see more. In the act, his injured limb came in contact with the barrier and made him grimace in pain. The drug the Terran medical worker had shot into it was wearing off.

Since he had made a slight noise already, Gerson crawled along about ten feet until he was just beside the head of the stairs. He made himself quiet to listen.

103

Somewhere below, two of the embassy staff were talking cautiously. It might be a good time to catch them unawares. He rose and took a step toward the stairs.

A voice that sounded artificially loud spoke in one or another of the lower chambers. It had a slight echo, making it nearly impossible for Gerson to determine the direction. The Terran who had ducked into the room on the left appeared, raising a weapon of some kind.

Gerson blazed a rocket in his direction. The slim missile, the length and thickness of the two top joints of his thumb, left a smoky trail just above the stairway railing and blew a large hole in the wall beside the doorway where the staff man had been standing. Somehow, the fellow had leaped back in time to avoid the flying specks of metal and plaster.

Gerson knelt behind the balustrade again, shaken by the sense of new pain, and wondering at its source. He concentrated. After a moment, he felt the wetness trickling down his left side. Some small object had grazed the flesh; and he realized that it must have been a solid pellet projected by the weapon of the Terran at whom he had shot.

He knew that the Terrans had more dangerous weapons than that, but had been confident that they would dare nothing over-violent here within their own building. The pistol used against him must be an old-fashioned one or a keepsake. Possibly it was a mock weapon built for practicing at a target. He seemed to remember vaguely having handled such a thing in the past.

He strained after the fleeting memory, clenching his teeth with the effort, but it was gone. So many memories seemed to be gone. All he was sure of was that he must get out of here with those papers.

He checked the upper hall again, before and behind. He looked across the open space for the Terran hiding like himself behind the balustrade, but could not find him. It might or might not be worthwhile to send a shot over there at random. If he missed, he might at least scare the fellow.

The loud voice with the mechanical sound to it blared out from below.

"Gerson!" it called. "Gerson, throw down your weapon and stand up. We can see where you are. We want to help you."

Gerson showed no reaction. Analyzing the statement, he reminded himself that one Terran had shot him. Not very seriously, it was true, but it was not in the nature of help. Either the voice lied or it had no control over the individual who had fired at him.

He did not blame it for the presumable untruth, since
104

he was not deceived by it. It would be preferrable to kill the man who had shot him, but he must bear in mind that his main task was to get out of the building.

"Gerson!" called the voice again. "We know you are injured. You are a sick man. We beg you to drop your weapon and let us help you!"

Gerson wondered what the voice meant by the expression "sick."

It was possible that someone had seen him wounded by the last shot. Or did they mean his sore limb. It occurred to him then that the blood that had run out and dried on the right side of his face must be clearly visible. The Terran he had killed back along the corridor had flung a small ceramic dish at him, and Gerson had been slow in raising his injured limb to block it. The whole side of his face was sore, but the skin of his cheek no longer bled so it was a matter of opinion whether he was sick on that account.

The voice must mean the last wound, when it called him sick. That meant that the Terran he had shot at was the voice or that there was another Terran in the room with him. Gerson did not think that any of the others could have seen. Some doubt at the back of his mind struggled to suggest an oversight, but he knew of none.

He peered once more between the balusters, and this time he saw a motion, a mere shadow, across the way. Instantly, he stood up and launched a rocket at the spot. It streaked on its way and exploded immediately against one of the uprights. Gerson regretted fleetingly that it had not gone through and struck against the wall beyond, which would have accounted for the skulking Terran with a good deal of certainty. As the baluster disintegrated, leaving stubs at top and bottom, Gerson started down the stairs.

Yells sounded from below. He threw one leg up to mount the stair railing, leaned back along it, and let himself slide. The rocket pistol, waving wildly at arm's length in his left hand, helped him to balance. He reached the landing at the middle of the stairs in one swoop.

The human at whom he had shot reappeared in the same doorway. Gerson rolled to his left, felt both feet hit upon the landing, and let go another missile. It was too late; the Terran had not even lingered to fire back. It seemed almost like a feint to distract.

"*Gerson!*" blared the mechanical voice.

"Gerson! Gerson!" shouted other voices.

They came from many directions, and he was unable to comprehend them all. He had reached a point near the bottom of the stairway, running three steps at a time, when

105

a louder yell directed his attention to the doorway on his right. The figure of a Terran showed there.

Without breaking his stride, he whipped his left hand across his body and fired a rocket. He had a glimpse of the figure dodging aside before the smoke and dust of the explosion told him he had nicked the edge of the doorway.

It seemed to him that he must have shot the Terran as well, and he let his eye linger there an instant as he reached the floor of the hall. Thus, he saw the figure reappear and was in position to fling two more shots with animal quickness.

The figure was blown straight backward this time, but Gerson had time to realize that there had been no head on it when it had been thrust out.

His first shot must have done that. All told, he had wasted three missiles on a dummy.

Then the loop of rope fell about him, and he knew why he had been lured into facing this direction. He tried to bring the rocket pistol to bear on the three Terrans running at him from behind the stairway. The fourth, at the end of the rope, heaved Gerson off his feet.

He crashed down upon his sore limb, letting out a groan at the impact. One of the runners dove headlong at him, batting at the pistol as he slid past on the polished floor. Gerson felt the weapon knocked out of his grasp. It rattled and scraped along the floor out of reach, but he kicked the one who had done it in the head.

Two of the Terrans were trying to hold him down, now. He got the knife from his mouth into his left hand, let a Terran see it, then bit him viciously on the wrist. The Terran let go, and Gerson found it simple to knee the remaining one in the groin. He rolled over to get a knee under him, pushed himself up with the fist gripping the knife, and saw Terrans running at him from all directions.

One of them had a broad, white bandage on his head. Gerson recognized him as the medical worker. The man carried a hypodermic syringe.

Unreasoning terror swept through Gerson. He knew that he must, at all costs, avoid that needle.

He whirled around to slash at the men coming up behind him. The nearest fell back warily.

"Put it away, Gerson," he said. "We don't want to hurt you, man! Why, you're half dead on your feet."

"What's the matter?" asked another, more softly. "We can see that you're not normal. What did those bastards do to you?"

Gerson looked from side to side, seeing them closing in but unable to spot an opening for a charge.

"Just listen to me a minute," said the medical worker. He made the mistake of holding the hypodermic out of sight this time, too late. "Gerson, talk to me! Say something! Whatever the trouble is, we'll help you."

It was the only opening.

Gerson took a carefully hesitant step toward him, then another. He held up his damaged limb.

"Yes, your wrist is broken," said the Terran. "I was going to put a cast on it for you, remember. Now, just relax, and we'll take care of—"

He saw Gerson's eyes and leaped back.

The knife swept up in a vicious arc that would have disemboweled him.

Without wasting the motion, Gerson slashed down and left at another as he plunged forward. The point grazed an up-flung arm, drawing a startled curse from the victim.

"Tackle him!" shouted one of the Terrans.

"Careful! He's already hurt bad enough," cautioned another.

Gerson tried to feint and throw his weight in the opposite direction, but his legs would not obey him. He recovered from the slip only to have one of the men push him from behind.

Someone clamped a tight hold on his left forearm as he staggered. A moment later they twisted the knife out of his grasp and bore him to the floor. He kicked ineffectively and then caught one of them by surprise with a butt.

The man recoiled, blood spurting already from his nose. He brought his fist around despite warning yells, and clipped Gerson on the temple.

"Hold him, dammit!" shouted someone. "Get that rope over here. Do you want to kill him? Just hold him still."

"*You* try it," invited one of those holding Gerson pinned.

"I think he's weakening," said another. "Watch out—he may be playing possum."

The talk seemed to come from far away. Gerson felt them tie his ankles together. They hesitated about his hands; one was injured. One voice suggested tieing his left wrist to the stairway railing, but it was decided that they could watch him well enough as long as he could not run. The weight lessened as those pinning him arose to look to their own bruises. Gerson was vaguely surprised to discover that all of them were off him. He still felt as if great weight were holding him pressed against the floor. He found it difficult to catch his breath.

They had taken the papers from his shirt, he noted. One

107

of the Terrans passed them to a man in a dark uniform, who began to leaf through them worriedly.

A Terran came in through the front door.

"Have you got him?" the newcomer asked. "That helicopter is still floating around up there. I've been watching it for half an hour with the night glasses. They sure as hell are waiting for something."

"And there isn't anyone else in this neighborhood they could be interested in," said a deeper voice. "Well, Mac-Lean, what did you let him get his hands on from your secret file?"

Gerson rolled over very quietly and started to drag himself along the floor. He had actually moved a yard before they noticed him.

They were gentle about turning him on his back again. The discussion about the papers was dropped while the medical worker cut his shirt away from the bleeding wound in his side. Hushed comments were made, but Gerson paid no attention. He was concerned with the fact that one of the Terrans had planted a foot between his legs, above the rope around his ankles, so that he was quite securely anchored to the spot.

"Looks like a broken rib besides," said the Terran examining him. "Do you think we could get him upstairs?"

"I'm no doctor," said the deeper voice, "but even I can see you'd never make it in time."

The voice came closer, though the vision in Gerson's eyes was blurring.

"Tell me, boy, what happened? How did they make you do it? What do they want?"

"Gerson!" said the man in the dark uniform. "Did you know what you were after when you took these papers?"

He was a dark blur to Gerson, who felt as if the weight on his chest had been increased. His lips were dry. He thought it would be nice to have a little water, but could not find words to ask.

The deep voice was flinging a question at the dark blur.

"Why, no, sir," said the Terran with the papers. "Nothing important at all. Just a few old shipping lists, a record of the planetary motions in this system that anybody could obtain, and an article on shortcuts to learning the Yoleenite language. I think I had the batch lying around the top of my desk."

"Why did he take them?" someone asked.

"Damned if I know. You fellows had me scared to death. From what you said, I thought he must have pinched the deadly top secret code and my personal address book to boot!"

"Simmons!" shouted the deeper voice. "Are you getting this? Are you making a tape for Terra? Oh . . . right out, eh? Scrambled, I hope—it's not the kind of thing to publicize to the galaxy."

The mechanical voice boomed in the background. Gerson paid it no attention.

He felt the doctor's hands touching the old injections and heard the man swearing. Whoever was holding his left arm was actually squeezing and stroking his hand. The taste of failure was in his mouth.

"That's what they must have started with," said the doctor. "In the end, they put an awful mental twist into him, poor guy."

"I told you they were up to something," said the dark blur. "Those little bastards had big ideas, but they won't catch us napping with any more spies, conditioned or not! Now maybe they'll read my reports on Terra."

Gerson opened his mouth to breath better. He rolled his head from side to side on the hard floor. Somewhere deep inside him, a little, silent voice was crying, frightened. He had failed and there would be no other chance.

The little voice took leave of its fear to laugh. *They* had not let him remember how to read.

And so he died, a tall, battered Terran lying on a hard floor and grinning faintly up at the men who had helped him die.

SIXTEEN

IN THE COMMUNICATIONS ROOM OF DEPARTMENT 99, Westervelt could actually hear people around him breathing, so hushed was the gathering. Someone was leaning on his shoulder, but he was reluctant to attract attention by moving.

Static sounds and the clicking and humming of various mechanisms about the room suddenly became unnaturally noticable. Glancing this way and that, he discovered that the entire staff had drifted in during the transmission from Yoleen. There were at least two people behind him, to judge by the breathing and the weight on his shoulder. So intense had been the excitement that he did not remember anyone but Smith arriving.

He saw better to the left than to the right, and became conscious of his eye again. Westervelt had drawn up his chair behind and to the left of the operator, and Smith had perched himself on the end of a table behind Joe. Beside the chief stood Simonetta, with Beryl behind her. Parrish was to Westervelt's left, so he concluded that Lydman and Pauline must be behind him. The grip on his right shoulder felt small to be Lydman's, but he could not see down at the necessary angle because of the puffiness under his eye.

The broad-shouldered, stocky man on the screen moved to the stairway and looked up straight into their eyes.

"Is this still going out to Terra, Simmons?" he asked.

He had dark hair with a crinkly wave in it, which permitted him to appear less disheveled than the men about him or standing over the body of Gerson. He pulled out a large white handkerchief to wipe the streaming perspiration from his face.

"Yes, sir," answered the voice of the distant operator. "You're looking right into the concealed pickup. I'll switch the audio from Terra to the loud speaker system, and you can talk to them."

Westervelt glanced at the other men in the embassy on Yoleen. Several of them obviously suffered from minor injuries. All of them wore expressions of tragedy.

One man in his shirtsleeves was standing with his shoulders against the base of the stairway, head thrown well back, trying to staunch the flow of blood from his nose. Another, with his back to the lens, knelt beside the body of Gerson. A couple of others, looking helpless, were lighting cigarettes.

"I suppose you saw the end of it," the man on the stairs said.

Smith cleared his throat and leaned over Joe Rosenkrantz's shoulder.

"We saw," he answered. "I . . . is there any doubt that he's dead?"

The man on the stairs looked to the group around the body. The doctor shook his bandaged head sadly.

"As much from strain and exhaustion as anything else," he reported. "The man belonged in a hospital, but some uncanny conditioning drove him on. In the end, his heart gave out."

The stocky man turned back to the lens.

"You heard that. Except for one man who didn't know at the time what was going on, we did the best we could. I'm Delaney, by the way, in charge here."

Smith identified himself, and agreed that Gerson had looked to be unmanageable.

"Do you think you can find out what they used?" he

ısked. "I gather that you never got anything out of him ʒince the time you picked him up. Did that part of it go ıccording to plan?"

"Oh, yes," said Delaney. "We even got back the little orch we sent him, the way you plotted for us. It looked ısed, too; but now I'm wondering if they let him cut his ᴡay out."

"I wouldn't doubt it," said Smith gloomily. "I'm afraid we lidn't look very bright on this one. We seem to have under-ʒstimated the Yoleenites badly. There isn't too much informa-ᴊion on them available here."

"Nor here, to tell the truth," said Delaney. "Which re-ninds me—our Captain MacLean has been after me for a ong time to put more pressure on the D.I.R. about that. ᴊould you duplicate your tape and send them a copy? It ᴠould save us another transmission, and you might like to ıdd your own comments."

Smith promised to have it done. He also offered, to sooth ᴊaptain MacLean, to send an extra copy to the Space Force.

There seemed to be nothing more to say. The scene on he screen blanked out, as the distant operator spoke to ᴊosenkrantz on audio only from his own shot-up office. Then ᴊ was over.

Westervelt, aware that the pressure on his shoulder was ʒone, looked around. Lydman had his arm about a shaken ᴊauline. The ex-spacer's expression was blank, but the hard-ıess of his eyes made the youth shiver. For a second, he ᴊhought he detected a slight resemblance to the man who ıad come bounding down the stairs on Yoleen, leaving criss-ᴊross trails of rocket smoke in the air.

That's crazy! he thought the next instant, and he lost the ᴊesemblance.

He blinked, fingered his tender eye, and looked around ᴊt the others. Everyone was subdued, staring at the blank ınd quiet receiver or at the floor. Westervelt was surprised to ʒee that Beryl was crying. She raised a forefinger to scrub he tears from her cheek.

Hesitantly, Westerevlt took the neatly folded handkerchief ᴊom his breast pocket and held it out.

Beryl scrubbed the other cheek, looked at the handker-ᴊhief without raising her eyes to his, and accepted it. She ᴊlotted her eyes, examined the cloth, and whispered, "Sorry, ᴡillie. I think I got make-up on it."

Smith stirred uncomfortably at the whisper. He stood up ınd spoke one short word with a depth of emotion. Then ᴊe kicked the leg of the table to relieve his feelings.

Rosenkrantz swiveled around in his chair, waiting to see

111

if any other calls were to be made. Smith took a deep breath.

"You'll make copies of the tape when you can, Joe?"

"Sure," said the operator, sympathetically.

"Well," said Lydman, at the rear of the group, "that's another one lost. Tomorrow we'll open a permanent file on Yoleen, as Pete suggests."

"Yes, I imagine they'll give us more business," agreed Parrish.

Lydman growled.

"I'll give *them* the business next time!" he threatened. "Well, that kind of damps the pile for tonight. I don't know about the rest of you, but I'm in no mood now to be clever."

Smith straightened up abruptly.

"Now . . . now . . . wait a minute!" he spluttered. "I mean, we all feel pretty low, naturally. Still, this wasn't the main . . . serious as this was, we were trying to push on this other case, to get a start anyway."

Here we go again, thought Westervelt. *Shall I try to trip him up if anything happens, or shall I just get out of the way?*

He recalled the man in the embassy on Yoleen, holding a stained handkerchief to his bloody nose, and measured the size of his own with the tip of a forefinger. On the other hand, if there should be a melee, it would certainly cover a little item like a puffy eye. He wondered if he would have the guts to poke out his head at the proper instant, and was rather afraid that he would.

Parrish was murmuring about sticking to the job in hand, trying to support Smith without arousing the antagonism of an open argument. Lydman seemed unconvinced.

"Why don't we all have a round of coffee?" suggested Simonetta. "If we can just sit down a few minutes and pull ourselves together—"

Smith looked at her gratefully.

"Yes," he said. "That's the least we can do, Bob. This was a shock to us all, but the girls felt it more. I don't believe any of them wants to hit the street all shaken up like this. Right Si?"

"I *would* like to sit down somewhere," said Simonetta.

"Here!" exclaimed Westervelt, leaping up. He had forgotten that he had been rooted to the chair since before the others had crept into the room during the transmission from Yoleen.

"Never mind, Willie," Simonetta said. "I didn't mean I was collapsing. Come on, Beryl, let's see if there's any coffee or tea left."

"Wait for me," said Pauline. "I've got to take this phone off the outside line anyway."

112

Smith stepped forward to plant one hand behind Lydman's shoulder blade.

"I could use a martini, myself," he called after the girls. "How about the rest of you? Pete? Willie?"

Parrish seconded the motion, Westervelt said he would be right along, and trailed them slowly to the door. He paused to look back, and he and Joe exchanged brow-mopping gestures.

The rest of them were trouping along the corridor without much talk. He ambled along until the men, bringing up the rear, had turned the corner. Then he ducked into the library.

He fingered his eye again. Either it was a trifle less sore or he was getting used to it. He still hesitated to face an office full of people and good lighting.

"There must be something around here to read." he muttered.

He walked over to a stack of current magazines. Most of them were technical in nature; but several dealt with world and galactic news. He took a few to a seat at the long table and began to leaf through one.

It must have been about fifteen minutes later that Simonetta showed up, bearing a sealed cup of tea and one of coffee.

"So that's where you are!" she said. "I was taking something to Joe, and thought maybe I'd find you along the way."

Westervelt deduced that she had phoned the operator.

"You can have the coffee," she said, setting it beside his magazine. "Joe said he'd rather have tea this time around."

Westervelt looked up. Simonetta saw his eye and pursed her lips.

"Well!"

"How does it look?" asked Westervelt glumly.

"Kind of pretty. If I remember the ones my brothers used to bring home, it will be ravishingly beautiful by tomorrow!"

"That's what I was afraid of," said Westervelt.

Simonetta laughed. She set the tea aside and pulled out a chair.

"I don't think it's really that bad, Willie," she told him. "I was only fooling."

"It shows though, huh?"

"Oh . . . yes . . . it shows."

"That's what I like about you, Si," said Westervelt. "You don't ask nasty, embarrassing questions like how it happened or which door closed on me."

Following which he told her nearly the whole story, leaving out only the true origin of the quarrel. He suspected that

113

Simonetta could put two and two together, but he meant to tell nobody about the start of it.

"Ah, Willie," she said with a grin at the conclusion, "if you had to fall for a blonde, why couldn't you pick little Pauline?"

"I guess you're right."

"Now, don't take *that* so seriously too! Beryl's a good sort, on the whole. In a day or two, this will all blow over. Come on with me to see Joe, then we'll go back and say you got something in your eye."

"But when?"

"Oh . . . during the message from Yoleen. You didn't want to bother anybody at the time, so you foolishly kept rubbing until it got sore."

"That's all right," said Westervelt, "but Beryl knows different."

"If she opens her mouth, I shall personally punch *her* in the eye!" declared Simonetta.

She giggled at the idea, and he found himself grinning.

They went along the corridor to deliver the tea to Rosenkrantz, and then returned to the main office. An air of complete informality prevailed, a reaction from the scene they had witnessed. There was a good deal of wandering about with drinks, sitting on desks, and inconsequential chatter.

No one seemed to want to talk shop, and Westervelt guessed that Smith was just as pleased to be able to kill some time. He himself quietly slipped around the corner to his own desk, where he propped his heels up and sipped his coffee.

Westervelt listened as Parrish and Smith told a few jokes. The stories tended to be more ironic than funny, and no one was expected to laugh out loud.

Pauline, from her switchboard, buzzed the phone on Simonetta's desk, since most of those present had gravitated to that end of the office. Smith looked around in the middle of an account of his struggles with his radio-controlled lawn mower.

"Want to take that, Willie?" he said, with a bare suggestion of a wink.

Westervelt lifted a hand in assent. He climbed out of his chair and went to the phone on Beryl's desk, where he would be as nearly private as possible.

"Who is it, Pauline?" he asked when she came on.

"It's Joe. He wants to talk to Mr. Smith."

"Give it here on number seven," said Westervelt. "The boss is talking."

Pauline blanked out and was replaced by the communica-

114

tions man. Rosenkrantz showed a flicker of surprise at the sight of Westervelt.

"Smitty's in a crowd," murmured the youth. "Something up?"

"Not much, maybe," said the other. "A message came in by commercial TV. I guess they didn't think it was too urgent, but I'll give you the facts if you think Smitty would like to know."

"Hold on," said Westervelt. "Let's see . . . where does Beryl keep a pen?"

He dug out a scratch pad and something to scribble with, and nodded.

"One of our own agents," said Joe, "named Robertson, signed this. You've seen his reports, I guess."

"Yeah, sounds familiar."

"It says, after reading between our standard code expressions, that two spacers and a tourist were convicted of inciting revolution on Epsilon Indi II. They gave the names, and all, which I taped."

"That's practically in our back yard," said Westervelt. "Maybe he just wants to alert us, but the D.I.R. ought to be working on that publicly. Sure there wasn't any hint it was urgent?"

"No, and like I said, it came by commercial relay."

"Okay. The boss has enough on his mind at the moment. Let's figure on having a tape for him to look at in the morning. I'll find a chance to mention it to him, so he'll know about it. All right?"

"All right with me," grinned Rosenkrantz. "If anything goes wrong, I'll refer them to you. Be prepared to have your other eye spit in."

He cut off, leaving Westervelt with his mouth open and his regained aplomb shaky. The youth waited until he caught Smith's eye, and shook his head to indicate the unimportance of the call. He wondered if he ought to take time to phone downstairs for a report on the situation. It did not strike him as worth the risk with all the people in the same room.

He saw Beryl strolling his way and rose from her chair.

"That's all right, Willie," she said calmly, setting her packaged drink on the desk. "I just wanted to give you back your handkerchief."

She produced it from the purse lying on her desk and said, "Thanks again. I'm sorry about the make-up marks."

"Forget it," said Westervelt.

"I'm sorry about the eye too," said Beryl, raising her eyes

for the first time to examine the damage. "It . . . doesn't look as bad as Si said."

"Well, that's a comfort, anyway. I got something in it and rubbed too hard, you know."

"Yes, she told me," said Beryl. "To tell the truth, Willie, I didn't know I could do it."

"Aw, it was a lucky swing," muttered Westervelt.

"Yes . . . I, well . . . you might say I was a little upset."

"I'm sorry I started it all," said Westervelt. "How about letting me buy you a lunch to make up."

Beryl shrugged, looking serious.

"I don't mind, if we make it Dutch. It was as much my fault. I hope we're both around to go to lunch tomorrow. It gives me the creeps."

"What does?" asked Westervelt.

"The way Mr. Lydman looks. Something about his eyes . . ."

Westervelt turned his head to stare across the room, wondering if the worst had occurred.

SEVENTEEN

JOHN WILLARD SET A BRISK PACE THROUGH THE streets of First Haven, as befitted a conscientious public servant. Maria Ringstad kept up with him as best she could. When she lagged, the thin cord tightened around her wrist, and he grumbled over his shoulder at her. Naturally, she carried her bag.

He had explained that they would have been most inconspicuous with her walking properly a yard behind him. Anyone would then have taken them for man and wife or man and servant—had it not been for her Terran clothing.

"To walk the street with you in that rig would attract entirely too much attention," was his explanation. "The only thing we can do is use the public symbol of restraint, so that everyone will know you are a prisoner."

"What good will that do? Won't they still stare."

"It is considered improper, as well as imprudent. No law-abiding citizen would wish to risk being suspected of a sympathetic curiosity about a transgressor."

"You make it sound dangerous," said Maria, holding out her hand obediently.

116

Anything to be inconspicuous, she had thought.

Now, turning a corner about three hundred yards from the jail, she had to admit that the system seemed to be working. The Greenies whom they met were nearly all interested in other things: a shop in the vicinity, another Greenie across the street, a paving stone over which they had just tripped, or the condition of the wall above Maria's head.

Willard led her to the far side of a broader avenue after they had negotiated the corner that put them permanently out of sight of the jail. Maria tried to recall the scanty information he had whispered to her against the outside wall of the prison.

There had been time for him to tell her he was sent by the Department of Interstellar Relations of Terra to get her out, since it had proved impossible to alter the attitude of the Greenie legal authorities. Maria was not quite sure whether he was really the prison officer he said he was, in which case he must have been bribed on a scale to make her own "crime" ridiculous, or whether he was an independent worker friendly to the Terran space line, in which case the payment might more charitably be regarded as a fee.

She knew that he planned to deliver her to a spaceship due to leave shortly. There had been no opportunity for her to ask the destination.

To tell the truth, she reflected, *I don't care where it is. Anything would be a haven from Greenhaven!*

She began to amuse herself by planning the article she would write when back on Terra. "How I escaped from Paradise" might do it. Or "Prison-breaking in Paradise." Or perhaps "Greenhaven or Green Hell."

Whatever I call it, she promised herself, *I'll skin them alive. And I'll find a way to send the judge and the warden copies of it, too!*

Maybe, she pondered, it might even be better to stretch it out to a whole book and get someone to do a series of unflattering cartoons of Greenie characters.

The cord jerked at her wrist. She realized that she had fallen behind again, and made an apologetic face at Willard when he looked back.

"Don't do that!" he hissed. "They'll wonder why I tolerate disrespect."

"Sorry!" said Maria, shrugging unrepentantly. "You take this pretty seriously, don't you."

"You'd better take it seriously yourself," he growled. "It's your neck as much as mine!"

He glared at a young Greenie who had glanced curiously from the opposite side of the avenue. The abashed citizen hastily averted his eyes. Willard gave the cord a significant twitch and strode on.

They turned another corner, to the right this time, and went along a narrow side street for about two hundred yards. Waiting for a moment when he might meet as few people as possible, Willard crossed to the other side. A little further on, he led the way into what could almost be termed an alley.

Willard stopped.

"Now, we are going into this small food shop," he informed Maria. "You would call it a cafe or restaurant on Terra. It will seem normal enough for an officer to provide his charge with food for a journey, so that will be reasonable."

"Is the food any better than what I've been getting?" asked Maria.

"It doesn't matter. We won't stop there, since it would be impolite to inflict the sight of you upon honest citizens at their meal. I shall request a private room, and the keeper will lead us to the rear."

"Humph! Well if that's the way it is, then that's the way it is. So in the eyes of an honest Greenie I'm something to spoil his appetite. What can I do about that?"

"What you can do is keep that big, flexible, active mouth of yours *shut!*" declared Willard. "Otherwise, I shall simply drop the end of the cord and take off. You can find your own way out."

"I'm sorry," apologized Maria, a shade too meekly. "I promise I'll be oh-so-good. Do you want me to kneel down and lick your boots? Or will it be enough if I open a vein in the soup?"

"It will be enough if I get out of this without committing murder," mumbled Willard. "Now, the expression is fine; just wipe that grin off your mind and we'll go in!"

He pulled her along the few yards to the entrance of the food shop.

He opened the door and entered. Maria followed at the respectful distance.

There were half a dozen Greenies eating plain, wholesome meals at plain, sturdy tables and exchanging a plain, honest word now and then. The sight of the cord on Maria's wrist counterbalanced the sight of her lascivious Terran costume, and they kept their eyes on their food after one startled glance.

A Greenie woman stood at a counter at one side of the food shop, and Willard made known his desire for a private dining room. A man cooking something that might have been stew looked around from his labor at a massive but primitive stove to the rear of the counter. Maria thought that he took an unusual interest in her compared to what she

118

had been observing recently. It rather helped her morale, and she thought she did not blame the man if the counterwoman were his wife.

The latter now came from behind her little fortress and led the way to a door at the rear of the shop. Willard followed, and Maria trailed along, restraining an impulse to wink at the cook. She was conscious of his analytical stare until the door had closed behind her.

Willard seemed to have nothing to say to the Greenie woman, and Maria relented to the point of heeding his request to be silent. All this made for a solemn little procession.

They walked along a short hall, and the Greenie woman opened another door to a flight of stairs. What surprised Maria was that the stairs led down. She shrugged—on Greenhaven, they had their own peculiar ways.

She was more puzzled when, at the bottom of the steps, they seemed to be in an ordinary cellar. The light was dim, and she did not succeed in catching the look on Willard's face. She began to wonder if she might wind up buried under a basement floor while he spent his ill-gotten bribe.

Then the Greenie woman pulled aside a large crate and opened another door. To pass through this one, they all had to stoop. Marie realized that they were then in the cellar of another building. The blocks of stone forming the walls looked damp and dirty.

They proceeded to climb stairs again, and to traverse another hall. Maria thought they ended up going in a direction away from the street. The woman led them through a small, dark series of rooms, and finally into one with windows set too high in the walls to see out. There she halted and faced Willard.

The Greenie prison official dropped the cord and reached into an inner pocket of his drab uniform. He withdrew a thick packet of Greenhaven currency. The numbers and units were too unfamiliar for Maria to guess at the value from one quick glance; but the attitude of their hostess suggested that it was substantial. Willard handed it over. Maria decided it was time to set down her bag.

The woman went immediately to a large chest in a corner of the room and opened it. She set aside a mirror she took out of the chest, then began to pull out other objects. There was a case which she handed to Willard and a great many articles of clothing that were probably considered feminine on this world.

"The point is," Willard said in low tones, "you are going

119

to have to have proper clothes to look natural on the street. See if that dress will fit you."

Maria took the thing distastefully, but it looked to be about the right length when she held it up against her. The Greenie woman nodded. She added a sort of full-length flannel slip and a petticoat to the dress.

"Now I know why the Greenie women look so grim" said Maria. "It would be almost worth dying to stay out of such a rig."

"Hold your tongue!" said Willard.

Maria made a face.

"Present company excepted, of course!" she added.

"Change!" ordered Willard. "We have no time to waste."

He took the mirror and the small case to a rude table under one of the windows. He opened the box so that Maria caught a glimpse of the contents, which looked like an actor's make-up kit.

The Greenie woman joggled Maria's elbow and spoke for the first time.

"I must not be long, or it will be noticed," she hinted.

"Give her your clothes to burn and get into the others," said Willard, bending over the table with his back to her. "As soon as I get myself fixed here, I'll change your face too."

Maria looked about in a manner to suggest that she hoped they knew what they were doing. The Greenie woman waited. Maria reached up and began to unbutton her blouse.

She dropped it across her bag. The woman picked both of them up, and waited. She looked a trifle shocked at the sight of the thin slip when Maria unzipped her skirt and hauled it over her head. By the time the slip followed, she was standing with downcast eyes.

Maria eyed the broad back in the drab uniform as she unfastened her brassiere. This would make a good story someday, but to tell it in the wrong company might be to invite catty remarks about her attractiveness. She could think of other men who might not have kept their backs so rigidly turned as did Willard. It was almost provocative.

She slipped down the brief panties, stepped out of them, and handed them over. The Greenie woman pointed silently to the shoes. Marie kicked them off, and they were added to the pile. She hoped that whatever was in the chest for footwear would not be too hard to walk in.

The Greenie woman thrust the flannel atrocity at her and left the room hastily. Maria watched the door close softly, then held the garment out at arm's length. It did not look any better. She took a few steps toward Willard.

I'll bet I could make him faint dead away, she thought

120

mischievously. *I'd love to see the look on his face if . . .
well, why not? I will!*

"She's gone," she announced in a low voice. "How do I get
into this thing?"

Willard looked around, and the look was nothing she
had ever seen before. His face appeared fuller in the cheeks,
his eyebrows were black and heavy, his nose high at the
bridge, and his whole complexion was darker.

He nodded at her gasp.

"Those papers I turned in for you won't last too long. The
estimate is that they will dissolve before tomorrow morning,
but they just might come apart sooner. If he sends out an
alarm, I don't want to be on the streets in shape to be
recognized."

"That's wonderful!" said Maria enthusiastically. "Are you
going to make me up too."

"Yes," said Willard. "Get into those things so I can start!"

Maria watched his eyes flicker to her breasts and then
sweep down the rest of her body. She thought he was taking
it very well, unless it was the make-up.

"Will you help me with this thing?" she begged. "I never
saw one before."

She held out the flannel garment with a helpless smile,
planting the other hand on her bare hip.

"*Will* you quit teasing, you little bitch!" Willard snapped.
"I'm no Greenie, if that's what you thought. You could get
us involved to the point of missing the ship."

Maria felt her eyes popping. A tingling, hot flush lit her face.
It spread back to her neck and crept down to her breasts.
She snatched the flannel sack to her and turned her back.

Somehow, she maneuvered it over her head. Then she
fumbled on the starched petticoat and topped the whole
with the dun-colored dress that fell chastely about her
ankles. Willard handed her a pair of low heeled shoes that
were only a little loose when she put them on.

He had her stand facing one of the windows while he
darkened her face and put a black wig on her. She looked
up at the window and stood very still.

"Now, listen!" said Willard. "You'll absolutely have to
stop blushing like that, or the color of the skin is going to
come all wrong!"

"I can't help it," she said meekly. Then she saw he was
laughing at her, and gave him a rueful smile. "Where did
all that modesty come from? It was the shock, I suppose."

right, it was funny. When we get out on the street

121

again, forget all about what's funny! Look like a serious Greenie!"

"Funny?" objected Maria. "I always thought I made a pretty fair showing in comparison to the local gals."

"Oh, you did, you did! One of the best showings I've ever seen."

He pressed a hand to each side of her waist, then slid them up her ribs until the weight of her breasts rested against his wrists.

"We'll talk about this again when we make it to the ship," he told her in a low voice. "Right now, it would be foolish to spoil this make-up."

He turned away after a long moment and returned the kit to the chest. They left by the same door by which they had entered, but Willard knew a short way out to a different street. Maria thought it must be the one outside the high windows. He set off at a businesslike pace.

They traveled about a quarter of a mile, counting several turns by which he sacrificed directness for sparsely peopled streets. The disguises must have been effective, for they drew no second glances. It was not until she saw the gibbet that Maria realized they were approaching the outskirts of the city.

"What—?" she began, sensing the reality of her plight for the first time.

"Quiet! Look the other way, if you must, but don't be obvious about it."

Several examples of rigid Greenhaven justice were on exhibit to a modest crowd. Three men and two women sat in stocks. They were not, apparently, subject to rock-throwing or other abuse, as Maria seemed to remember had been the custom on ancient Terra; but they were clearly unhappy and mortified. From the gibbet behind them swung the body of a hanged man. It appeared to have been there for some time. Maria wondered what *he* had done to corrupt the morals or the economics of Greenhaven.

What nearly made her sick was the sight of a party of two dozen children being guided on a tour of the place. One youngster whined, and was thoroughly cuffed by the Greenie in charge.

Then they were past, and Maria saw the high cyclone fence of the Terran spaceport. Willard took a look at her face. Seemingly satisfied, he explained that they had come to a section well away from the main entrance. He led her along the fence for perhaps a hundred yards, found a small gate, and unlocked it with a key produced from under belt. Maria, remembering their exit from the jail, surprised to feel a good-natured slap on the bottom as she stepped onto Terran land. There was another quarter-mile to go, but it was open land.

"We have it made now," said Willard, locking the gate behind them.

They by-passed the administration and custom buildings, and headed directly for the field elevator beside the waiting spaceship, ignoring the possibility of causing inquiries to be made by local eagle-eyes who might think they had seen two Greenies board the vessel.

"Willard, of the Department of Interstellar Relations," he introduced himself to a surprised ship's officer. "You've been told to expect Miss Ringstad?"

The officer, staring in bald disbelief at Maria's costume, admitted that the ship was more or less being held for her arrival.

"One thing was unexpected," said Willard. "I am exercising my authority to demand a cabin for myself as well. I have reason to suspect that my disguise had been penetrated, which, of course, makes it very dangerous for me."

"Of course," agreed the officer. "Let's go, by all means!"

"Yes," said Maria. "I want to get out of this awful rig."

"That's what I meant," said Willard.

There was no doubt that the influence behind Willard had held the ship for them. It rose as soon as they could reach a pair of tiny cabins. Later, after the first surge of the take-off, there were a number of delays stretching between minor course corrections.

Finally, it was announced over the public address system that because of precautionary checking of the course, there would be no spin to simulate planetary gravity for about two hours. Maria hoped that she would not be revealed as the cause to the disgruntled passengers.

She was still considering this and trying to disentangle herself from the acceleration net slung in the ten-foot cubicle they were pleased to call a cabin, when Willard arrived.

"I made friends with some of the crew," he announced. "Everybody likes to help out a D.I.R. agent. It must strike them as romantic."

"They should know," said Maria, thinking of the long, suspenseful walk through Greenhaven's streets.

"There was a stewardess who had extra slacks and blouse about your size."

"You must have a good eye," she told him. "Or think you have, anyhow. First, get me out of this thing. What with this Greenie outfit too, I might as well be in a straitjacket!"

He pushed himself over to the net and began to open the

123

zipper. She saw that he had taken time to remove his "Greenie" face.

Her first motion, when the net was open, sent her tumbling head over heels to the far bulkhead.

"Keep a grip on something," laughed Willard. "Here—I brought a small kit along. Let me fix your face."

She obediently clung to the anchoring shock springs at one end of the net and turned her face up so that he could work on the mask he had earlier painted on. His fingers were gentle, smoothing in the cream he had brought and rubbing off the make-up with lightly perfumed tissues. Maria closed her eyes luxuriously and thought how pleasant it was to be off Greenhaven.

"Was it very complicated, getting me out of there?" she asked.

"There were a lot of angles to think of," he answered, "but we pulled it off as slickly as I've ever seen done. Just strolled right out through them all. Things in this business don't often go that well to plan. There—now you look human again, just like when I started to put that face on you."

"Not exactly," smiled Maria, plucking ruefully at the native Mother Hubbard, which billowed hideously about her in the zero gravity.

"That's easily changed," Willard said, meeting her smile significantly. "See if you can find your way out any better than you did getting into it, while I sort out the clothes I got for us."

Between the reaction from the strain of the past few hours and a glow of gratitude toward her rescuer. Maria began to sense the stir of an emotion within her that took a few moments to recognize. It surprised her a little.

"Willard," she said lazily, "it's funny, but I feel just as if I'm falling in love with you."

"That's interesting," grinned the agent. "About time, too."

"I can't tell if my knees are weak," she went on, laying a hand on his shoulder to draw herself closer, "because I'm hanging in mid-air; but you always seem to be making me strip—and I find myself not minding."

"I don't mind either!" he assured her.

When his arm slipped around her waist and he kissed her, Maria was sure. She let her lips part gradually, trembling as the fever rose in her.

"Let me go a minute," she murmured.

Presently, after a few weightless contortions, the muffling Greenhaven flannels were sent swirling into a corner. Maria laughed softly as she set a bare foot against the bulkhead to launch herself back into Willard's arms.

124

EIGHTEEN

eyerything seem to sway?

Or was it the swaying that made his head hurt?

Taranto opened his eyes slowly. For two or three minutes, in the darkness, he did not understand what he saw.

Gradually, comprehension developed. He was on a litter again, and the bearers were descending a rough track into a shallow valley. There was no sign of the city or of any other landmark even vaguely familiar. Jagged rocks formed a ridge to his left, curving around to enclose the depression. Other rocky buttes, he saw through slitted eyes, projected from the barren rubble of the valley floor. There seemed to be little sand, unless it had blown down into the lower areas.

Cautiously, letting his head roll with the lurching motion of the bearers, he learned that another group was ahead. He thought they must be guarding Meyers. The red-uniformed officer marched just preceding Taranto's litter. That meant that there must be two soldiers behind, out of his view.

What now? he asked himself. *It was a good try, but it didn't work out.*

It seemed hopeless to attempt anything further until he found out where he was. Nor would it do any harm to learn *how* he was—they must have crowned him beautifully. He tried to move his arms and legs slightly without being obviously restless. Nothing felt broken. There was just the sore throbbing behind his left ear.

Were they taking him and Meyers further into the desert, to make sure they could properly be reported dead? Or was the party on its way back to the city?

Taranto moved about stealthily, as the litter heaved from side to side and bounced about with the efforts of his bearers to negotiate outcroppings of rock. He was surprised that his arms and legs were not tied. He wondered how long he had been out cold. Perhaps the Syssokans believed he really was dead from that spear across the skull.

You shouldn't have underestimated that guy just because you dropped him a few times, he told himself. *You caught on to the difference, but he learned it from you.*

From ahead and lower on the path came voices. There was a brisk breeze, but Taranto thought he could recognize Meyers giving vent to an outraged whine.

Wonder how much of a grudge they'll hold? he thought. *Some of them must be lumped up pretty good.*

He was beginning to locate a number of scrapes and bruises on his own sturdy frame. He wondered if it might be best to take things easy until they reached either their desert destination or the area outside the city, according to which way they were headed, and then offer to bribe the officer in charge. It would probably be too risky: he would have to rely on large promises, and they had already caught him in a crude whopper. Whatever the case, it would be unwise to open negotiations without finding out what the Syssokan commander looked like. Taranto seemed to recall pasting the fellow pretty thoroughly.

He caught a few words of Terran, blown back to him by a random gust. Meyers was complaining about being too tired to walk any farther. It did not sound as though he were making his point.

Of course! Taranto realized. *I must be in his stretcher. Mine was busted. Now the slob will put it on me for making him bump his rump along this trail!*

The image was not without humor. Contemplating it gave Taranto a momentary satisfaction.

Well, they knew Meyers was alive, even if they might not be sure about Taranto himself. Perhaps they were merely saving both Terrans for a longer jail term. Taranto hoped that the Syssokans had nothing more unpleasant in mind. The remarks he had used earlier in his attempt to bluff the officer could be used for inimical purposes by anyone who cared to point out that Syssokan knowledge of Terran physiology was scanty. Then what?

Taranto decided that he would be foolish to worry along that line at the present. What he needed was an idea for getting loose again. He speculated for a few minutes upon his chances of backtracking to the scene of his attempt at escape. Somewhere near there, in whichever direction it was, a spaceship should be landing.

If they ain't been and gone already, he thought.

In his supine position on the stretcher, he was able to see the sky without moving. That was why the distant trail of light was visible to him for some moments before any of the Syssokans could notice it.

I can't wait it out after all, he realized.

The ship would be heard presently, and the flare of its braking rockets would arouse the guards. Taranto peeked around again and saw that they were nearing the foot of the slope. Following the natural motion of the bearers, he let himself roll a little too far each time the litter swayed. The

126

Syssokans struggled to compensate while scrabbling for safe footholds on the hard, slippery surface.

In the end, one of them slipped. The litter crashed down. Taranto added a twist to the natural force of gravity, so that he rolled downhill.

The fallen bearer picked himself up, mumbling something in Syssokan that sounded remarkably belligerent. One of the others moved to recover the stretcher. Taranto kept on rolling.

At the first yell, he gave up the pretense and regained his feet with a lithe bound. For the next sixty seconds, he needed every last smidgin of concentration to escape taking a fatal spill on the sloping rocks.

Hurtling downward in great leaps, he was forced to hurdle large rocks because his velocity prevented him from changing course by even a foot. Once he skidded, thinking his time had come. Near the bottom, where the incline curved to meet the horizontal, he did go down, ploughing up a spatter of loose chips and pebbles.

He was up and running again without quite knowing how. A dark shape loomed up before him, a rock twice his height. Before passing it, he took the chance of looking back.

The litter party was in a state of confusion. The officer and two soldiers were bounding after him, slanting away on a more reasonable path. One Syssokan was still in the process of picking himself up, and most of the others were either milling about or just beginning to heed their leader's shouts to follow Taranto.

The intention of yelling to Meyers flashed across his mind but he dismissed it as being useless. A hasty glance in the opposite direction showed him the fire trail settling behind another ridge to his right front. The valley bore a certain resemblance to a meteor crater.

Taranto sprinted past the huge rock and bore right toward the distant ridge. He would try to locate the ship if and when he reached the ridge. The immediate necessity was to keep out of the clutches of the burial party.

Running in the starlit darkness was risky, as he soon found. The ground was strewn with occasional patches of loose stone, traps of nature suitable for tripping the unwary or causing a sprain. The only thing that kept Taranto reckless was the sounds of pursuit behind him.

He had gone about two hundred yards when he realized that some of the rock-scattering noises came from his right more than from behind. The Syssokan were better runners than he, and used to the local terrain besides. He could not tell whether they had seen the trail of the spaceship or, if so, whether they connected it with him.

But they know enough to head me off, whichever way I go, he thought.

He came unexpectedly to a patch of sand, and swore as he felt his speed slacken. A desperate glance over his shoulder revealed no pursuers, though he knew they were there somewhere. He could see two runners who had flanked him on the right fifty yards off; and these forced him into bearing away from his desired course.

Instead of passing to the right of a tall outcropping of rock ahead, he turned left. It took him farther from the direction of the spaceship, but there was no help for it. He floundered over a low dune of sand and then was out of it and running on flat ground. He circled to the left of the hill, hearing a howl from the rear.

Must have seen me against the open valley, thought Taranto. *They sound closer than I like.*

He ran on, scanning the shadowed rocks towering over him for a place to climb. It was a foregone conclusion that the two flankers would be on the lookout for him as he came around the hill.

At last he thought he saw a way up, a sloping ledge leading to a small plateau before the rock reared higher in a sheer cliff. Taranto scrambled over a waist-high boulder and made for the opening. Up he went, on hands and toes. The rock was ridged, but in the wrong direction, and he slipped to hands and knees twice before he was up.

He slowed to a quick walk as he reached the level expanse. It was ten or twelve feet above the valley floor and curved off to the right around the base of the cliff. Taranto was panting by now, but his main reason for slowing was that he wanted to make less noise until he spotted the two Syssokans he expected to meet.

The broad ledge he was following dipped, rose a few feet, and dipped again to less than ten feet above the level ground. Taranto flattened himself suddenly.

The two Syssokans came loping along the shadowy edge of the outcropping, spears at the ready. From around the cliff sounded a call. The first soldier threw back his head to answer. As the howl left his throat, and masked the noise of the Terran's scrambling, Taranto launched himself upon the back of the second.

They went down with a thump upon hard rocks. Taranto, saving his ribs from being caved in by fending himself off from a jagged rock with his forearm, kicked out and caught the downed Syssokan in the belly. As the soldier subsided,

he Terran snatched up the spear and rose to face the other
)ne.

It had all gone so fast that the leader was just turning
)ack. Perhaps he thought merely that his companion had
:allen, but the stocky silhouette of the spacer disabused him
)f that idea. He advanced with the point of his spear
weaving about menacingly.

"You think you're good with that stick, eh?" growled
Taranto. "Well, try this for something different!"

Gripping his spear near the head, he swung the heavier
)utt like a bat, putting as much power into it as he could.
:t was crude, but he knew better than to try to match skills
with a soldier trained to the use of the weapon.

The butt cracked resoundingly against the shaft of the Sys-
iokan's spear, tearing it from the grip of his leading hand.
Taranto's own hands were numbed by the shock. He dropped
iis spear and slid inside the Syssokan's one-handed grip
)efore it could be reinforced. The feint of a left hook to
he belly made the soldier relinquish his weapon completely
ind grapple with the spacer.

Taranto found his left arm entwined with the right of the
Syssokan. He tried twice to punch to the body with his free
land but was smothered. Before he could think of it himself,
he Syssokan stamped hard upon his toes.

"Bastard!" spat the spacer.

He butted, successfully but profitlessly. He rabbit-punched
wice with his right hand, reaching around under the soldier's
irmpit. Only when he gouged at a large, black eye did
he defending arm come up.

Taranto set his feet and banged three times to the midsection, getting plenty of body twist into his motion.

He found himself holding a very limp Syssokan, who slid
down as the spacer stepped back.

Taranto sucked in a gasping breath. He staggered aside to
pick up the spears, feeling better now that he was armed, no
matter how primitively.

He had hardly straightened up when he saw the officer
round the edge of the little butte, a mere fifty feet away. The
Syssokan hesitated at the sight of the Terran standing over
two of his soldiers, and Taranto threw one of the spears.

The trouble was that he did not know how to handle one.
A spear, after all, was not standard equipment on a space-
ihip. The point twisted away from the target, and much of
he force went into a slow spin. The officer hissed a dis-
lainful comment and caught the weapon out of the air
with one hand.

Taranto stooped for a rock, which he hurled with more

effect. It shattered with a fine crack against the cliff near enough to the Syssokan to make him throw himself behind a boulder for cover. Taranto left him in the middle of a yell to his soldiers and sprinted off into the open valley.

Carrying the spear did not help matters much, but he thought the Syssokans might regard it as a more dangerous deterent than he knew it to be in his untrained hands. The next time he looked around, he saw that he could rejoice in a splendid lead of two hundred yards. On the other hand, the officer now had a numerous group with him, and would probably get organized at last. Taranto slowed to a jog, to save himself against the time when they should begin to catch up.

"Taranto!" said a small voice.

He broke automatically into a dead run, without even looking around.

"Wait, Taranto!" called the little voice. "Look up, for the spy-eye!"

The spacer slowed as understanding burst upon him. He looked back and saw a spark of light gaining on him. It arrived and hovered over his head.

"It may still work," the voice informed him. "The ship is down. I told them what happened, and they're putting up a helicopter. Where's Meyers?"

"I don't know," said Taranto. "Back on the ridge, I guess. Look, I can't just stand here until that 'copter comes. I'll be a pincushion."

"Head for that hill ahead about a quarter-mile," said the voice from the little flyer. "I'll guide them there."

The Syssokans were running now, spreading out in a well-drilled manner. Taranto boosted himself into high speed again.

The hill ahead was more toward the center of the valley. If the pursuers were aware of some connection between his flight and the position of the spaceship, they would be satisfied to have him heading away from the ridge enclosing the valley. Taranto hoped that they would not worry enough to turn on a burst of speed, for he was convinced that they could outrun him.

He was right—he reached the steep slopes of the hill with a bare fifty yards left of his lead, and he was on the point of foundering at that. His knees buckled for an instant as he hit the first rise, and he saved himself from pitching on his face only by thrusting out the butt of the spear he carried.

Somehow, he made it another fifty feet up the slope, hearing the voice beside his ear say, "To the right, Taranto! Head for that flat spot! Here comes the helicopter."

He wiped salty sweat from his eyes with the back of one

130

land and looked up. A large, quietly whirring shape shadowed
he stars. It dropped rapidly toward him as a howl broke out
behind him.

Taranto took the spear in both hands, holding it at one
end, and sent it whirling end over end at the closing Sys-
iokans. The whole center of the group dropped flat to let
t swish over their heads.

Before they could rise, the helicopter reached Taranto. It
came down so fast it bounced against the ground. Someone
held out a hand to Taranto and yelled to him to jump. He
vas hauled into an open cockpit. Someone took a deathgrip
in the waistband of his pants and he felt the helicopter climb.

He wiggled around until he could get his knees under him.
There were two spacers in the cockpit of what was obviously
in auxiliary craft from a spaceship. One of them, a very long-
eared type with a narrow head, looked as if he had been
born in some stellar colony. The other had a broad, bland
ace of an oriental Terran.

"Where is the other one?" asked the latter.

Taranto crept between the seats to which they were
trapped before answering, for there were only chains at the
open sides. He got his bearings, and directed the long-eared
pilot to the ridge where he had rolled out of the litter.

It nearly broke his heart to see them reach it in less than
a minute.

"There may be guards with him," he warned. "Maybe
he took off too."

"We shall see," said the broad-faced spacer.

He ran a spotlight along the ridge, stopped, and brought
t back to bear upon a lonely figure. Meyers stood up and
vaved. No Syssokan was in sight; the officer must have taken
hem all with him.

He knew what he was doing, thought Taranto. *The guy's
till here.*

The helicopter eased down to hover over a large rock.
Meyers climbed laboriously upon it and was hauled aboard.
Taranto squeezed himself back behind the seats to make
oom.

"It's about time you got here," puffed Meyers. "I'm worn
out."

Taranto said nothing as the craft rose in the air and
wooped off toward the spaceship. Someday, Meyers would
sk how he had gotten away from the Syssokans. When it
happened, Taranto swore to himself, he would *show* the slob.

131

NINETEEN

IT WAS TWENTY AFTER EIGHT WHEN WESTERVELT found himself back at the communications room with Smith. Rosenkrantz had alerted them to a message coming in from Syssoka.

"They didn't expect to hit us during office hours," he explained, "but as long as you're here, I thought maybe you'd like to get it fresh."

Smith had told the girls to pass the word to Lydman and Parrish, and Westervelt had followed him down the hall with the feeling that he had displayed his eye under the good lighting long enough. Now they listened as a slim, brown-haired man with a faintly scholarly aura completed his report on the escape of Louis Taranto and Harley Meyers, spacers.

Joe Rosenkrantz was fiddling with an auxiliary screen and murmuring into another microphone.

". . . so it was a rather close call, even though the formula you sent us appears to have worked perfectly," said the scholarly man. "I have not been able to determine exactly what caused the delay on the part of the Syssokans, since it seemed imprudent to display my little flying spy-eye where it might be seen, or even damaged."

"Maybe you can pick up some rumors in the future," suggested Smith. "If you do, we'd appreciate hearing them, to add to our file and make the case as complete as possible."

The transmission lag was much less than that occurring with Trident. The D.I.R. man on Syssoka agreed to forward any subsequent discoveries.

"Those spacers you contacted are already heading out-system," he told Smith. "I think they did a nice, clean job. It was too bad that they were seen at all, of course, but it will be news to me if the Syssokans drop around with any embarrassing questions."

"Well, there is a large foreign quarter there," Smith recalled. "Why should they suspect Terrans, after all?"

"Oh, they will, they will. They suspect everyone; but they must know so little that I feel sure I can bluff them. I can prove that I was here at the official residence all day."

"Good!" said Smith. "Just in passing, I take it that no one was much hurt?"

The man on Syssokan grinned briefly.

"No one on our side," he said, "although I understand the

prisoners were suffering some from exhaustion and dehydration. This Louis Taranto seems to be quite a lad. There is reason to believe that he killed two or three of his guards with his bare hands—at least I saw the burial party carrying bodies with them as they marched the rest of the way back to the city."

Smith laughed.

"I'll have to add a note opposite his name and contact him. I could use a field agent like that! Well, my operator tells me I have another call coming in. Thanks for your work on this."

"A pleasure," said the man on Syssoka. "I really didn't expect to contact you directly; my relative-time atlas must be a little old."

"No, it's just that we never sleep, you know," quipped Smith, and signed off.

He looked around, saw that it was Parrish who had entered, and added, "At least, it *looks* as if we'll never sleep. I'm getting tired of it myself."

"So is everybody except Joe, here," said Parrish. "A com man isn't normal anyway."

"You gotta learn not to let all this stuff coming through bother you," said Rosenkrantz wisely. "If I soaked up all these crazy calls, I'd have nightmares every day. As it is, I'm as normal as anybody when I leave here."

"You haven't been with us long enough," said Smith. "What else do you have there?"

"There was a routine memo to make a check with the planet Greenhaven," said Rosenkrantz. "I cleared it when a good time came. The D.I.R. station there pretended not to know what I was talking about."

"What?" yelped Smith. "Don't tell me we goofed on another one!"

"I don't think so," said Rosenkrantz. "While you were talking to Syssoka, a spaceship named *Vulpecula* called, said there was reason to believe the Greenhaven D.I.R. was locally monitored."

"Tapped or the scrambler system broken," said Parrish. "What does this ship want to talk about."

"The Ringstad case."

"Joe, godammit, who says you're normal?" demanded Smith. "I bet we've sprung another one! Two in one night—we're coming out with a good average after all. Get them on the screen before I pop my tanks!"

Westervelt listened to the transmission from the spaceship. Without the help of a planetary relay at the far end, it tended to be a trifle weak and wavery, but the essentials

133

came through. He left Smith and Parrish patting each other on the back and went back to tell the girls about it.

They clustered around him in the main office, even Pauline leaving her cubicle for a moment and keeping one ear pointed at the switchboard inside.

"You should have heard Smitty conning her out of writing us up for the news magazines," said Westervelt. "She seems to be pretty famous in her line."

"What was she like?" asked Simonetta.

"She looked blondish, but the color wasn't coming across too well. Not bad looking, in a breezy sort of way. The agent that sprung her had to skip too, because he thought the Greenhavens—they call them Greenies—had spotted his disguise."

"Oh, boy!" breathed Pauline. "The cops must have been hot on their trail!"

"Either that, or he wanted to go along with her for other reasons," said Westervelt. "They seemed kind of chummy."

"Can they do that?" asked Beryl. "I mean, without orders, and all that?"

Westervelt grinned.

"I don't know," he admitted, "but he's doing it. He can't go back now. Anyway, Smitty simmered down fast and promised a draft for expenses would be waiting for him when the ship made planetfall. Technically, the D.I.R. ought to pay, because it turns out the guy is on their rolls and was only working with us temporarily."

Simonetta nodded wisely.

"You watch our boss," she predicted. "He'll have this man on our lists. He always gets free with the money when he sees a good prospect from the main branch. Even if they stay in the honest side of the outfit, they cooperate with the back room here."

Smith walked in with Parrish, beaming. His eye found Westervelt.

"Willie," he said, "make a note, and tomorrow look up the planet Rotchen II. I have to send credits, and I didn't want to say into wide, wide space that I didn't know where it is. Bad for the department's prestige!"

He looked about genially.

"I see you've told the news," he commented. "It was a lift for me too. We haven't done too badly, after all. Won two, lost one—damn!—and one is still a stalemate."

"Anyone tell Bob?" asked Parrish quietly.

They all exchanged searching glances. Smith began to lose some of his ebullience. After a moment, he turned to Pauline.

134

"Buzz his office!" he said in a preoccupied tone.

Westervelt tried to subdue a mild chill along the backbone as Pauline gave Smith a wide-eyed look and slipped into her cubbyhole.

He couldn't have phoned downstairs, he reassured himself. *Pauline would say all the lines were busy, or cut off or something. But what if he looked out a window?*

Smith had sauntered over to the center desk, where he waited beside the phone. It seemed to be taking Pauline a long time.

"Check with Joe," advised Parrish. "Then try around the other rooms. Ten to one he's in the lab."

"Has anyone seen him in the last half hour?" asked Smith.

Westervelt pointed out that he had been the chief's company in the communications room. The girls had not seen Lydman, but admitted that he might have gone past in the corridor without their having noticed.

"Yeah, he doesn't make much noise," Parrish agreed.

Smith had a thought. He moved toward his own office, paused to jerk his head significantly toward Parrish's, and opened his own door. Parrish went over past Beryl's desk and thrust his head into his own office. Lydman was not in either room.

"Mr. Smith!" called Pauline in a worried tone. "I'm sorry, but I can't seem to reach him."

"Oh, Christ!" said Parrish. "He isn't talking again!"

He did something Westervelt had never seen that self-possessed man resort to before this evening. He began to gnaw nervously upon a knuckle. He saw the youth staring, and snatched his hand from his mouth.

Smith glowered unhappily at the floor. Westervelt thought he could hear his own pulse, so quiet had the office grown.

The chief backed up to the unpleasant decision.

"We'd better spread out and wander around until someone sees him face to face," he said. "If he wants to be let alone, let him alone! Just pass the word on where he is."

Westervelt volunteered to go down one wing while Parrish took the other. As they left, cautioned to take their time and act natural, Smith was telling the girls to open the doors to the adjacent offices again and keep their ears tuned, in case Lydman should come looking for him or Parrish.

Westervelt turned right past the stairs, and went to the door of the library.

It will be perfectly natural, he told himself. *We made out on two cases. I just want to tell him about it, in case he hasn't heard. Why the hell don't they get that cable fixed? They want their bills paid on time, don't they?*

135

He could hear the newcasts now, about how tough a job the electricians faced, and how tense was the situation. Westervelt decided he would not listen.

He opened the door to the library casually and sauntered in. The pose was wasted; Lydman was not there.

Westervelt went on to the conference room on this side, and found it empty as well. He looked in on Joe Rosenkrantz, who, from the door, appeared to be alone. Just to leave no stone unturned, he retreated up the hall to the door marked "Shaft" and poked his head inside. He had to grope around for a light switch, and when he found it was rewarded with nothing more than the sight of a number of conduits running from floor to unfinished ceiling. A little dust drifted down on him from atop the ones that bent to run to outlets on the same floor.

"Well, nobody can say I overlooked anything," grumbled Westervelt.

He went back to the communications room. Rosenkrantz was listening in on some conversation from a station on Luna that was none of his business.

"Any sign of Lydman around here?" asked Westervelt.

"Not since the Yoleen brawl," grunted Rosenkrantz. "That's a good-looking babe running that Lunar station. Why can't we dig up some messages for them?"

"I'll work on it," promised Westervelt halfheartedly.

He walked quietly around the corner past the power equipment. No Lydman. The next step was the laboratory. He looked at his watch, then leaned against the wire mesh partition for a good ten minutes. Let Parrish cover the ground, he decided.

In the end, with no sign of Parrish or Lydman, he opened the door and stepped into the dark laboratory. He made his way cautiously ahead, thinking that Lydman was probably in his office. Feeling his path with slow steps, and carefully avoiding the possibility of tipping over any of the stacks of cartons, he had progressed to the center of the large chamber when the lights went on.

Westervelt felt as if he had jumped a foot, and the blood pounded through his veins.

Gaping around with open mouth, he finally met the eye of Pete Parrish, who stood half inside the doorway to the corridor, his hand still raised to the light switch.

They both relaxed. Parrish smiled feebly, with less than normal dispay of his fine teeth. Westervelt contented himself with passing a hand across his forehead. It came away damp.

"Well," said Parrish, "where was he?"

Westervelt closed his eyes and groaned.

136

"You're kidding," he said. "Please say you're kidding! It's too late in the day to fool around, Pete."

Parrish looked alarmed. He strode forward, letting the door close behind him. Westervelt, finding himself shivering in a draft, went to meet him.

"I'm not kidding at all," said Parrish. "Did you look everywhere? Are you sure?"

"I even poked into the power shaft," retorted Westervelt. "Were you in his office?"

"Naturally. I checked everything, even the men's room."

They had wandered back to the corridor door, peering about the laboratory to make sure no one could have concealed himself on the floor under a workbench, or behind a pile of cartons.

Parrish opened the door, and they stood puzzling at the empty hall.

"He wasn't even taking a shower," said the elder man.

Westervelt brooded for a moment.

"Did you say *everywhere?*" he insisted.

"Well . . . everywhere he would have any call to go."

They stood there, passing the buck silently back and forth between them. At length, Parrish said, "I'll just look again in his office and the other two rooms, in case he *was,* and slipped out behind me."

Westervelt watched him run lightly up the hall to each of the doors. Parrish's expression, as he returned slowly, was something to behold.

"I'll go," said Westervelt grouchily.

Parrish put a hand on his arm.

"No, that wouldn't look natural. I'll phone Smitty to send one of the girls down."

"Better phone him to send two," suggested Westervelt.

"Yeah," agreed Parrish. "That's even more natural. Watch the hall while I buzz them."

He went into Lydman's office. Westervelt leaned in the laboratory doorway, feeling depressed. After some delay, he sighted Simonetta and Beryl turning the far corner with their pocketbooks in hand. Neither one looked particularly pleased, but their expressions lightened a bit at the sight of him.

"You there, Pete?" murmured Westervelt.

"Right at the door," whispered Parrish from inside Lydman's office.

The girls clicked in muffled unison along the hall. Beryl paused at the entrance to the ladies' rest room. She raised her eyebrows uncertainly at Simonetta. The dark girl threw Westervelt a puzzled shrug, then pushed past Beryl and went inside. The blonde followed almost on her heels.

Westervelt waited. When he thought he could no longer stand it, Parrish hissed, "How long are they in there, Willie?"

"I don't know," said the youth, "but maybe we'd better—"

The door opened. Simonetta anl Beryl walked out, staring quizzically at the two men, who had taken a few steps toward them.

"What is this gag?" asked Simonetta. "There's no one in there. Who would be in there?"

Parrish swore luridly, and none of them seemed to notice.

"It *can't* be!" he exclaimed. "You're sure?"

"Of course we're sure," said Beryl.

"What if the power came on and we didn't notice?" mused Parrish. "He wouldn't just leave and not tell any of us, would he?"

"You know him better than I do," commented Beryl. "I'm beginning to wonder, from what you told us on the phone, if he jumped out of a window somewhere. I know it's a terrible thing to bring up—"

Westervelt stopped listening to her. He was remembering the draft he had felt, twice now, in the laboratory.

TWENTY

WESTERVELT WATCHED THEM WALK UP THE HALL. He thought of going back into the laboratory to find the open window. In his mind, he could see the straight, twenty-five story drop down the side of the dark tower to the roof of the larger part of the building.

He recalled having looked down once or twice. The people down there had paved patios outside their offices. A hurtling body would . . .

He shook the thought out of his head and hurried to catch up to Parrish and the two girls.

They trouped into the main office and took turns in telling Smith the story. He flatly refused to believe it for about five minutes. Ultimately convinced, he told Pauline to check Rosenkrantz by phone every ten minutes.

"If we're wrong," he said, "it's unfair to have him sitting down there all alone. Bob might somehow have outsmarted us, but if he did it to this extent, it means he isn't safe on the loose!"

138

Westervelt noticed that Simonetta was looking pale. He wondered about his own features. The eye would probably stand out very picturesquely.

"I don't believe it," he said when the others had all fallen silent.

They looked at him, hoping to be convinced.

"He isn't that kind," said Westervelt. "All right, you tell me he had a hard time in space and it left him a little off; but this doesn't sound like the direction he would go off in."

"What do you mean, Willie?" asked Smith intently.

"Well . . . maybe he'd run wild. Maybe he'd get desperate and blow something up. I could see him taking a torch to that door and burning anybody that tried to stop him . . ."

He paused as they hung on his words.

". . . but I *can't* see him quitting!" said Westervelt. "If he was that kind, he never would have gotten back to Terra, would he?"

Smith snapped his fingers and looked around.

"Sure, sure," he said. "I don't know what I was thinking up in my imagination. We've all heard Bob utter a threat now and then, when some bems out in deep space broke his own private law, but no one ever heard him even hint at suicide."

He grinned ruefully, and added, "I should have thought of it myself—I had to review his application and examinations when he came to us."

"Some days," said Parrish, "are just too much. Nobody's fault."

"Then, in that case," said Westervelt, "there was one little thing I noticed."

He told them about the open window. Who would keep a window open with the building air-conditioning operating as perfectly as it did?

Smith fell to running his hands through his hair again.

"Now, let's *think!*" he muttered. "There must be some logical explanation."

Logical explanations, Westervelt thought, *are always the reasons other people think of, not me.*

He found a space to sit on the edge of the empty desk. Simonetta leaned beside him, and Beryl wandered over to the window of the switchboard cubicle to listen as Pauline checked Rosenkrantz.

She shook her head to Smith's inquiring look.

Then Lydman strolled through the double doors.

"What's the conference about?" he asked.

Beryl let out a shriek. Her back had been to the corridor

139

when she jumped, but she came down facing the other way.

Everyone stiffened.

Lydman stood quietly, regarding them with nsiderable calm.

After a moment, Beryl tottered back to lean ag ' st the glass of Pauline's window. She pressed one hand t her solar plexus, looking as if she might fold up at any brea .

"Oh," she gasped. "Oh, Mr. Lydman . . ."

He examined her with a clinical detachment.

"Doesn't someone have a tranquilizer for her?" he asked. "I don't usually scare pretty girls."

"Oh, no, no, no . . . it's just that . . . I mean, everyone was worried about you," stammered Beryl.

"Why?" asked Lydman. "Don't you think I can take care of myself?"

For the first time, Westervelt noticed the curiously set expression on the ex-spacer's face. He had until then been too busy watching Beryl and trying to calm his own nerves. He could not be certain, but it seemed as if Lydman's forehead displayed a faint sheen of perspiration.

"Of course you can, Bob," said Smith. "We were—"

Beryl, nearly to the point of hysteria in her relief, got the ball away from him.

"We were worried about the elevator being stopped," she babbled. "And the door—you'll never believe it, Mr. Lydman, but the door to the emergency stairs wouldn't open!"

Westervelt thought he heard Parrish swear, then realized it had been his own voice. He started to step in front of Simonetta.

Parrish was moving slowly in Lydman's direction, trying to look at ease but looking tense instead.

"Dammit!" shouted Smith. "Beryl, you're *fired!*"

It did not seem to register on anybody, Beryl least of all. Lydman was confounding them all by standing quietly. His face tightened a little more at the news, but it did not seem to be the expression of a man who had just taken a bad jolt.

"I know," he said. "I looked at it a couple of times after I saw the blackout downstairs."

Smith regarded him warily.

"How do you feel, Bob?" he asked.

"You know how I feel," said Lydman.

He let his gaze wander from one to anoth r of them. Westervelt felt a chill as the handsome eyes loo ed through him in turn, but accepted the comforting realiza on that the stare was about as usual.

Beryl was the picture of a girl afraid to brea e out loud,

140

but the others relaxed cautiously. Smith even planted one hip on the corner of Simonetta's desk and tried to look casual.

"You seem to be doing pretty well," he said. "We were thinking of looking in the lab for something to cut the latch with, but it might have been waste motion. They should be getting the power on any minute now."

"I think . . ." Lydman began.

"Oh, I guess we could find something in the lists," pursued Smith. "If you'd rather we look . . . ?"

"I have several things we could use," said Lydman.

He walked into the office proper and looked about for a chair. Westervelt stepped back of the center desk and brought him the chair of the vacationing secretary. Lydman sat down beside the partition screening the active files opposite Simonetta's desk.

"In fact," continued the ex-space, "I got them out when I was trying to figure how much that door would stand. Then I decided that would only raise a commotion."

Westervelt watched him with growing interest. Now that he had the man at closer range, he was sure that it was a tremendous effort of will that kept Lydman so relatively calm. The man seemed to be seething underneath his tautly controlled exterior.

"What did you think of doing?" asked Smith carefully.

"Oh, I dug out a better gadget, one that would do *me* more good, anyhow," said Lydman. "It's a little rocket gun attached to a cannister of fine wire ladder."

"Wire ladder?" repeated Smith.

"Yeah. About six inches wide at the most. I opened a window and shot it up to the flight deck. Say—did you know some hijackers stole all three of our 'copters?"

"Stole all three of . . ." Smith's voice dwindled away. When no one else broke the silence, he forced himself to resume. "Yes, I knew. What I would deeply appreciate, Robert, is your telling me how the hell *you* knew!"

He finished yelling. Westervelt thought that he looked at least as bad as Lydman. Anyone twenty feet away would have completely misjudged them.

"Just as I said," answered Lydman with his tight calm. "I shot this ladder to the roof and climbed up."

"You climbed up? *Outside the building?*"

"Of course, outside," said Lydman, for the first time showing a trace of snappishness. "I couldn't stand it *inside.*"

He looked around at them again, surprised that there was the slightest hesitation to accept his statement.

"We'll have to redesign that ladder, though," h said. "It's a mite too fine—cuts the hell out of your hands!"

He held out his palms. Across each were s eral welts. One, on his right hand, had apparently resum   bleeding stickily since Lydman had come in. He fumbled ut a handkerchief with his other hand and blotted it.

Smith held his hands to his head.

"I can't swallow it yet!" he groaned. "You fe l . . . uneasy . . . in here, so you go out a window ninety nine floors in the air—"

"Only twenty-four above the set-back, really   Lydman corrected him.

"It's enough, isn't it? So you go out, climb up to the helicopter roof, and *then* climb down again and b k through the window! And you pretend to feel better. I   ould have had a heart attack!"

"Who wouldn't?" said Westervelt.

The mere conception of what it must have bee like made him feel sick.

"As long as I know it's there," muttered Lydma . "As long as I know it's there. I can use that way any time Just don't anybody pull that little ladder down."

"Would . . . ?"

The meek little syllable came from Beryl, wh had now managed to stand without the support of the parti 'on.

Every head in the room swiveled to bear upo her. She gulped, and found part of her voice.

"Would there be an old martini lying around in e locker?" she asked. "I'm afraid to go for it myself becaus my knees feel as if they'll collapse at the first step."

There was a general outburst of laughter th t revealed the enormity of their relief. Parrish hurried over to put an arm around the blonde, and Smith himself w nt to the locker and opened it.

With the break in the tension, Beryl manag   to walk pretty well, perhaps with a little more swagger f the hips than usual, Westervelt thought. Smith found a dr· k for her, and insisted that Lydman have tea. The chief pul ed the tab himself and held the cup for the few seconds quired to heat the beverage.

Most of them, like Westervelt, had had too m ny coffees or sandwiches, and were content to sit down nd regain their composure. Westervelt was mildly surprised o see Parrish take a position behind Lydman and knead th big man's neck muscles to relax him.

"Did they tell you the news yet?" asked Smi . "We got two out—Syssoka and Greenhaven!"

142

"No!" said Lydman, managing a smile. "Tell me, but if I get up to leave in the middle, I'd rather you didn't stop me."

"Nobody is stopping anybody tonight!" said Smith, and fell to giving his assistant an account of Taranto and Meyers.

Westervelt got up quietly and padded into the switchboard cubbyhole.

"Lend me your headset, Pauline," he murmured, "and punch Joe's number."

"Sure," said the little blonde.

She left the screen off and kissed him behind the ear just as Rosenkrantz answered.

"Nothing personal, Willie," she giggled. "I just feel so relieved!"

"Who is it now?" demanded Rosenkrantz's voice. "You left the lens off, did you know that?"

"It's Willie, Joe. He came back and he's sitting down having tea."

"*Back?* Where was he?"

Westervelt told him.

Then he told him again and switched off. Joe, he thought, would have to live with it for a while.

When he stepped out of the cubicle, everyone was watching Smith narrate, with broad gestures, the flummoxing of the staid authorities of Greenhaven. The chief was not above calling upon Parrish for an estimate of the charms of Maria Ringstad that caused an outcry among the girls. Lydman smiled politely, but not from the heart. He was still quietly reserved.

Everyone was watching Smith. No one paid any attention to the redhaired man who drifted into the office area just as Westervelt squirmed past Pauline and stepped out of the switchboard room.

The youth blinked at the topcoat over the man's arm. He focused upon the wavy hair and reached for the man's shoulder to turn him around.

"Charlie Colborn!" he yelped.

Smith got it first.

"Well, now," he said, standing up. "If it's getting so everybody and his brother start parading through that door at this time of night, I'm leaving! Where's my hat, Si?"

Lydman had caught on almost as quickly, and was on his feet before the general whoop went up.

"I just want to phone my wife," said Colborn. "It's so late I might as well stay here the rest of the night. What's keeping all of you?"

They glared at him.

"The power's been on for fifteen minutes," he told them.

"I would have been up sooner, but that nut of a building manager insisted on running test trips with all the elevators before he'd let anyone come up."

Lydman had started for the elevator, in shirtsleeves as he was and carrying a cup of tea in one hand and a bloody handkerchief. There was no doubt that he meant to go home that way.

"BOB!" roared Smith. "All of you—*listen!*"

Lydman stopped but did not turn around.

"In the first place, Charlie," said Smith, "you are *not* going to call your wife from here unless you faithfully give the impression that you are all alone. If you slip, I'll swear to her I saw you picked up by two redheads in a helicopter and you had all the office petty cash with you."

"But—"

"Tell her the traffic was too much. Don't tell her we couldn't get to the street. That goes for everybody else too!"

"But . . . *why?*" Colborn got out.

"Why? You want the D.I.R. boys throwing this up to us every time I try to get money out of them for the bare necessities of our operation? We can get people out of dungeons on planets not even in the Galatlas, but can't even escape from our own little hideaway?"

"It never happened," Parrish agreed quickly.

"Damn' right!" said Smith. "Okay, Bob, push the button! Go with him, Willie! You girls—nobody in before noon tomorrow; we have an extra TV operator to take care of things."

"Look, I . . ." Colborn started to say as he stepped out of Westervelt's way.

"Aw, thanks for phoning in the first place," grinned Smith, punching him lightly on the shoulder. "Wait for me downstairs, Willie! We'll see what we can do about Harris tomorrow!"

"Appoint him an ambassador," muttered Westervelt, coming up behind Lydman as the elevator door slid smoothly open.

What an outfit! he thought to himself. *I'm going to apply for field duty, where you can get out among the stars and let someone else figure ways to keep you out of trouble.*

Somehow, incredibly, everyone but Colborn managed to catch the same elevator.